DEFENDER

-OF THE-

REALM

MARK HUCKERBY AND NICK OSTLER

DEFENDER
-OF THE-
REALM

SCHOLASTIC PRESS
NEW YORK

All rights reserved. Published by Scholastic Press, an imprint of Scholastic Inc., *Publishers since 1920*. SCHOLASTIC, SCHOLASTIC PRESS, and associated logos are trademarks and/or registered trademarks of Scholastic Inc.

The publisher does not have any control over and does not assume any responsibility for author or third-party websites or their content.

Library of Congress Cataloging-in-Publication Data available

ISBN 978-0-545-93666-8

10 9 8 7 6 5 4 3 2 1   17 18 19 20 21

Printed in the U.S.A.   23

First US edition, April 2017

Book design by Carol Ly

-For Anna and Melanie-

◄ TABLE OF CONTENTS ►

ONE

Breakout

Somewhere between five and eight. That was how many bones Alfie was sure he was about to break as he lost his grip on the drainpipe, fell ten feet, and landed butt-first in the flower bed outside the prison walls.

Alfie was skinny, with thick mousy-brown hair that always seemed to curl down over his face, no matter how much gel he put in it. His eyes were a deep sea green, which hit you more in person than it did in photos. Everyone said he got them from his grandmother. Alfie wiggled his toes and was happy to discover that he could still feel his legs. He sat up, rubbed the back of his neck, and wiped the mud from his watch. It was a little after nine thirty p.m. *Right on schedule.* He had planned this break-out down to the minute. If his calculations were correct, then he wouldn't even be missed for—

"STAY WHERE YOU ARE!"

Then again, Alfie's plans had a habit of going wrong. The gruff voice boomed down from the window he'd just climbed—well, *fallen*—from. By the time Alfie had scrambled to his feet, he could hear heavy footsteps somewhere inside the cell block, coming his way.

The Man in Black, thought Alfie. *There's no way he's stopping me this time. No way.*

Alfie sprinted across the lawn toward the street. Vaulting over a low brick wall, he caught a glimpse of the huge arch of Wembley Stadium glowing in the distance. As much as he hated the prison, he had to admit its position on a hill just outside London gave it some spectacular views. Alfie risked a look back, just in time to see the dark-suited, broad-shouldered man with neatly clipped hair hurdle the wall and tear after him.

"STOP!"

Alfie sped up, legs already on fire with the effort, as he flashed past cars parked along the narrow, tree-lined street. But the Man in Black was closing on him, fast.

"I SAID, STOP!"

Alfie skidded on a patch of leaves and veered into a park that had appeared to his left. He might not be as fast as his pursuer, but the night was on his side. He pushed through some bushes and crouched behind an oak tree. Pressing his face against the cold, wet bark, he ignored his desperate need to gasp down air.

Branches snapped nearby as the Man in Black

bulldozed his way through the scrub. Alfie stayed still and watched him barrel out of the trees, grumbling and cursing with every sapling that whipped across his face. Finally free of their grasp, the Man in Black spun around three hundred and sixty degrees in a desperate search for his prey, and then ran on in the opposite direction.

Alfie finally sucked in a super-sized lungful of air. *That was too close.*

A few minutes later, double-checking that no one was on his trail, Alfie crossed over the Station Road bridge. A train thundered below him on its way out of the city. Every night he would lie awake in his cell listening to the distant rumble from the tracks and dream about hopping onto a train car one day and just seeing where it took him. Mountains would be good, or a forest or lonely moorland. Alfie had always liked the wilderness. Somewhere remote where he could be himself and—

A bus trundled past, faces gazing blankly from the windows. Alfie snapped out of it. What was he thinking? There were too many cameras on the station, too many people. Besides, he had his mission. It was decided. He needed to focus.

Alfie picked up the pace, fished a crumpled baseball cap out of his jacket pocket, and pulled it over his head. The one thing that he'd learned about disguises over the years was that less is more.

Forget false beards and noses; the trick was not to draw too much attention to yourself. Blend in; be *inconspicuous*. It was Alfie's favorite word.

He hurried across the bridge and onto the bustling main street. It was a world away from his usual surroundings, but he was enjoying himself. It was just so good to be out. Alfie broke into a jog, sticking as much as he could to the shadows, avoiding the late-night shoppers who passed him by without a glance. And then suddenly, there it was in front of him: a modest little building with a bright neon sign in the window. His goal—the end to his quest. Alfie reached for the door handle and stopped in his tracks.

Snipers.

Half a dozen of them, sitting inside. They were dug in around a table, idly adjusting their telescopic lenses, no doubt swapping war stories as they waited for their target. For *him*. Alfie realized his mistake, but it was too late. He shouldn't have stopped walking; he should have just breezed past, not gawked like a dumb kid straight at the enemy. As bad luck would have it, one of the snipers—bearded and craggy, with all manner of equipment draped over his shoulders and shoved into a utility belt—glanced up and locked eyes with Alfie. He couldn't hear him through the glass of the door, but Alfie could read his lips well enough.

"THERE HE IS!"

Mission aborted.

For the second time that night, Alfie ran for his life. But this time there was nowhere to hide; the parade of shops was too well lit. And he was still tired from his footrace with the Man in Black.

Behind him, the snipers piled out of the building, readying their weapons, unhooking tripods, bringing scopes to their eyes as they gave chase.

Alfie plunged across the road, threading the needle between a bus and a cab. Horns blared and air brakes hissed. He couldn't afford to give them a clear shot. These were pros—all they needed was one split-second chance and he was history.

On the other side of the road, Alfie spotted an alleyway between a pub and a cell phone shop. He ducked down it, but there was no telling where it led, and he could hear the snipers' shouts not far behind. Then he saw it: large, square, and green, with a hinged rubber lid.

No choice.

Alfie hauled himself up and into the trash bin, slamming the lid down behind him. It stank of rotten food, and Alfie tried to pretend it didn't smell like someone had been sick into it as well. He froze as the heavy footfalls and breathless yells of the snipers approached. He closed his eyes and prayed. *Walk past, walk past.*

Footsteps came and went. Then . . . silence. They'd gone.

Alfie was desperate to escape his foul hiding place, but he forced himself to wait another full minute before he eased the lid up and peeked out.

FLASH!

Light exploded all around him as the bearded sniper took a clean head shot. Alfie screamed and flew back, a thousand supernovas in his eyes. He looked up, dazed, as the sniper leaned in for another shot, tearing back the trash bin's lid and pushing the long lens of his camera into Alfie's face.

"Say cheese, Your Highness!"

Prince Alfred Henry Alexander Louis, Prince of Wales and heir to the throne of the United Kingdom of Great Britain and Northern Ireland, stared up from the depths of the trash bin and gave the paparazzi photographer a big, sarcastic thumbs-up.

"Happy now?" Alfie couldn't even summon up much anger. This photographer was just doing his job.

"What do you think?" said the rat-faced little man. "Who wants a photo of the future king of England hiding in the trash? That'll be ten thousand quid, thank you very much." The photographer got a whiff of the bin's interior and recoiled. "Phwoar. Have you been sick in there, Your Highness?"

Suddenly the photographer was hauled off his feet. It was the Man in Black, otherwise known as Brian, Alfie's royal protection officer. For once, Alfie was pleased to see him.

Brian manhandled the indignant sniper away with one shove of his mighty palm. "That's enough—you've had your fun."

The photographer didn't put up much of a fight—one glance at Alfie's bodyguard told him that he was ex–Special Forces. But then, why bother? He'd gotten what he came for. He holstered his camera and sauntered off, pulling out his phone, no doubt to start the bidding for his exclusive snap of the prince in the trash.

Satisfied that the threat was gone, Brian turned back to Alfie and fixed him with a weary stare.

"OK, Brian, you found me. Your turn to hide. Shall I count to twenty?"

Brian sighed. He wasn't in the mood for Alfie's jokes tonight. "What were you popping out for this time? Curry? Fish and chips?"

"Pizza, actually. Ambrogio's does the best pepperoni in town."

"It also happens to be where all the paps go to eat every Thursday night." Brian snorted.

"You're annoyed with me, aren't you? Making you run around like that," said Alfie.

"I was. Until I saw you hiding in a trash bin—that's cheered me right up."

"Suppose it's back to prison, then, is it?" Alfie extended his hand.

But Brian backed off, holding his nose. "If you're talking about school, then, yeah, it is. Can't wait to see how you explain this one to the headmaster tomorrow," he laughed.

Alfie tried to clamber out of the garbage, but Brian pushed him back again.

"Hold up. You're not getting in my car smelling like that."

"I can't walk back," Alfie pleaded. "There'll be snipers everywhere by now."

Brian furrowed his brow and looked up and down the alleyway. "Good point. Hold your breath."

"Why?"

Alfie ducked as Brian slammed the lid back down over him.

"BRIAN!" Alfie yelled from the darkness.

"Put a sock in it. There's a good lad. You never know, you might get lucky and find some pizza in there."

The bodyguard grinned as he wheeled the bin off, whistling "God Save the King."

TWO

The Ceremony of the Keys

If this was the best the Tower of London could do, then she wanted her money back.

Hayley Hicks tucked a stray frizz of hair behind her ear and flipped her jacket collar up against the icy drizzle. She had no idea that in a matter of minutes, her life was going to change forever.

Hayley had been watching a soldier in a red tunic and tall bearskin cap holding a rifle and doing a whole lot of nothing for what felt like *decades*. Well, not exactly nothing: He was standing still, guarding a big oak gate beneath a hulking old tower. Hayley wasn't even sure the guy was blinking, and she spent a minute or two pretending she was in a staring contest with him before giving up. *All right, you win*, she thought, and sighed. This was no way for any self-respecting girl to spend a Thursday night: stuck with a bunch of tourists outside a moldy old castle, getting cold and wet. She wiggled her toes to make sure they hadn't dropped off, then stamped her feet for good measure.

"Stop fussing, child. It'll be worth it, you'll see." Hayley's grandmother scowled up from her wheelchair, pretending to be annoyed.

"It's all right for you, in your little cocoon on wheels," Hayley shot back. But she was smiling. "I'm dying of hypothermia here, Gran."

She'd made sure the wheelchair was packed with blankets before they'd set off for her gran's seventy-seventh birthday treat: a trip to the Tower of London to see the Crown Jewels. There was even a thermos, a spare pair of socks, and an extra-woolly hat in her backpack. Not to mention her gran's medication, all in neatly labeled bottles. It had taken Hayley the better part of three months to save up for today—lunch, tickets, and taxis that could take a wheelchair didn't come cheaply in London—but she was glad she'd done it. Hayley hadn't seen her gran so perky in years—she hadn't stopped her commentary about all things royal (her favorite subject of all time) and historic (second-favorite subject of all time) for the entire day.

But the best part of the trip was still to come. Hayley had secretly booked tickets for something called the Ceremony of the Keys. Tonight they would have the honor of being in the select group of tourists permitted to watch as the Crown Jewels were locked safely inside for the night. Hayley had never heard of the ceremony before she started doing her research, but her gran had practically leapt out of her chair when Hayley surprised her with the tickets.

"Seven hundred years, Hales! They've been stomping around locking this place up in the same way for seven hundred years—every night, come wind, shine, snow, or blow." Her gran had a weird saying for pretty much everything.

"Wow, really?" Hayley was only pretending to be interested, but her gran didn't notice.

"Well, that's a lie—they did miss one night in the war when a bomb landed there."

Hayley figured it would take more than a bomb to scare her gran. She'd emigrated from Jamaica in the 1950s, married a white man when everyone still thought that was somehow wrong, became one of the first woman Tube drivers, got a degree in history from the Open University at the same time, and generally packed more into her life than most people would ever manage. She was not a woman afraid to speak her mind, and Hayley just prayed they'd make it through the ceremony without her gran shouting out something "helpful" to the soldiers. She'd already made eyes at the guard at the doorway and said, "Hey, handsome, give us a twirl!" He'd stared back without blinking.

In fact, speaking of ceremonies, when was this thing going to kick off? Hayley glanced at her watch and—

"HALT!"

The sentry whipped his rifle from his shoulder, the bayonet glistening from the drizzle, and pointed it squarely at five new soldiers who were marching up to the gate. They stopped, as one. Three of the soldiers held their own rifles, while a fourth carried a lantern that cast an eerie glow up the high stone walls. The man they were escorting was short and tubby with a bushy ginger beard. Hayley would have called him a beefeater, but her gran whispered that his proper title was actually the chief yeoman warder and that, no, he wasn't wearing a dress; it was a tunic. His dress (tunic, whatever) was black with red trim and had the letters HR emblazoned on the front. Gran told her they stood for *Henry, Rex*—Latin for King Henry. The chief yeoman warder carried a sword sheathed under his belt, and from one hand dangled a bunch of long iron keys.

"Who comes there?" barked the sentry.

"The keys!" came the reply from somewhere under the chief yeoman warder's beard.

"Whose keys?"

"King Henry's keys!"

After seven hundred years, you'd think they'd

know that! thought Hayley, but she kept her mouth shut and looked to her gran, who was entranced, gripping the wheelchair armrests with tight little hands.

Satisfied, the sentry shouldered his rifle and stood at attention. "Pass, King Henry's keys, and all's well."

"Escort to the keys, by the center, quick march!" yelled the sergeant.

And off they went, ferrying the chief yeoman warder past the sentry.

Another beefeater had now appeared and was ushering the tourists under the arch of the nasty-sounding "Bloody Tower" and onto Tower Green, where they would witness the conclusion of the ceremony.

Its slick, wet cobbles lit only by a handful of lamps, the central courtyard looked quite different from the bustling square in which Hayley and her gran had eaten their sandwiches earlier that afternoon. An unseen raven croaked from the battlements. Hayley shivered. It was here, on the executioner's block only yards away, roped off and marked with a plaque, that several important men and women had lost their heads. Hayley's gran told her that the ghost of one of them—Anne Boleyn—was said to still roam the courtyard at night, carrying her own head!

The rest of the Tower Guard were waiting on the wide central steps. Hayley wheeled her gran to the front so she could see. The chief yeoman warder held his hat in the air and bellowed to the sky, "God preserve King Henry!"

"Amen!" shouted the guards in unison.

"Amen!" added her gran enthusiastically, drawing a ripple of giggles from the group. Hayley smiled and tried not to go red.

The clock tower chimed the hour—ten o'clock. Hayley had to admit, the precision of the timing was impressive. A bugler started playing, the lonely notes echoing off the high walls around them. The chief yeoman warder returned his hat to his head and hefted his big key ring as he took the last few steps toward the Jewel House door. *At least we're nearly done here*, thought Hayley. She was mentally preparing herself for the long taxi and train ride back home to their apartment.

"Wonderful, isn't it, Hales?" Hayley's gran whispered. "Really makes history come alive."

Hayley was just about to reply when things started to get monumentally strange.

A sound of rushing air, like the whine of a falling bomb, whistled across the courtyard, and a large, dark figure thumped onto the ground no more than forty feet from where they were standing. The impact was hard enough to make Hayley's teeth click together. Several soldiers dropped their rifles with a clatter. A middle-aged Japanese woman in the tour party shrieked and put her hand to her mouth.

Hayley peered at the figure that had just fallen to earth. It was crouched in the corner, unmoving. For a second she assumed a statue or some sort of hideous gargoyle must have come loose and fallen from one of the towers. A thought flashed through her mind: *Lucky no one was killed.*

Then the "gargoyle" moved. Rearing up to its full height, at least seven feet tall, it stood like a man, but was covered in thick, smooth, black scales. Its face was pulled taut into a thin, cruel snout, topped with a row of bony spikes. Its enormous hands and feet were tipped with vicious claws. Everything about it looked somehow fresh and not yet fully formed: slick and glistening, like some newborn monster. Hayley's mind was doing flips trying to make sense of what she was seeing—*a black lizard man.*

A young, gangly American tourist flicked through his guidebook and gawked at Hayley, bewildered. "Is this part of the show?"

The sergeant was the first to react—he stepped forward and leveled his rifle at the towering shape of what the internet would soon be calling the "Black Lizard."

"Who goes there?" His voice was neither as loud nor as confident as it had been only moments before.

The Black Lizard's head snapped round toward the sergeant, and for the first time, Hayley got a clear view of its eyes. The irises were deep red, while the pupils were long and black, like the dark slit of night behind a half-drawn curtain. The creature's intelligent, sinister gaze swept across her and the rest of the tourists like a searchlight. Hayley felt sick.

With an earsplitting shriek, the beast leapt toward the soldiers. It was as if a button marked GO! had been pressed, as everyone scattered. Screams erupted from the tourists as they barged past one another to get away. Gunfire filled the air as the soldiers unloaded at the Black Lizard. Hayley's head was spinning. *The guns are loaded!*

Sparks flew from the lizard man's scale armor as bullets bounced harmlessly off it. With another screech, it jumped ten feet through the air and smashed through the first-floor outer wall of the Jewel House, sending stone and splintered wood raining onto the ground outside.

Hayley grappled with her gran's wheelchair, trying to turn it toward the gate and safety, but the wet cobbles made it hard to maneuver at any speed.

"Get out, Hayley! Leave me here!" shouted her gran.

"Not a chance," replied Hayley.

A second almighty crash from the Jewel House made Hayley look back. The Black Lizard reemerged through the hole in the wall and thumped to the ground again. It was holding a cluster of glittering objects in its huge claws—a golden scepter, an ornate sword, and a jewel-encrusted crown. Hayley recognized them; they had lined up to look at them through reinforced security glass earlier that day: the Crown Jewels.

Is that what this is—a heist? A smash-and-grab for the Crown Jewels? she wondered.

But then the Black Lizard did something very peculiar. It tossed the treasures aside as if they were junk. Hayley remembered her gran saying that some people thought the Crown Jewels on display in the Tower were fakes, and that the originals were kept hidden away somewhere secret. Was that why the beast had discarded them? Could it tell, somehow?

A yell rang out, and Hayley was astonished to see the chief yeoman warder rushing at the monster, his sword held high. The Black Lizard turned and cocked its head ever so slightly. Maybe the thing wasn't expecting to see a short, round, beardy guy in a red-and-black miniskirt square up to it, but that's what was happening. Hayley wanted to yell out, "Let it go! Don't be a hero!"

but somehow her voice seemed to have stopped working.

The deflection, when it came, was savage and short. The Black Lizard didn't even move its feet. It simply backhanded its attacker in the chest. There was a sickening crunch as the brave beefeater was thrown high into the air, landing with a dull thud right next to Hayley and her gran. Gasping, Hayley watched as the man's eyes swam, seeking a focus they wouldn't find. His bloodied lips parted as he exhaled his final words.

"God . . . save . . . the king."

This couldn't be real. Nothing about it made sense. Next to Hayley, her gran was opening and closing her mouth wordlessly while the gangly American tourist filmed the scene on his phone, using the wheelchair as cover. Hayley was just about to snap at him to find another hiding place when things went up another level, into the realm of the truly weird.

The unmistakable whinnying of a horse echoed around the courtyard walls. Hayley was suddenly hopeful. *Has someone sent in the cavalry?* High above the battlements, a ghostly horse was *hovering*. The horse didn't have wings or jets or any visible sign of what was keeping it aloft, but there it was, a translucent horse with plate armor covering its head and flanks, hanging in the air high above her. As it

dived toward the ground, Hayley saw that someone was riding it. A knight. His sleek armor was as
gleaming white as the Black Lizard's scales were
impenetrably dark.

Even though she didn't yet believe what she
was seeing, Hayley knew who this was: the Defender.
All she needed now was the Loch Ness Monster
and the Yeti to join the party and she'd have the
full set. Because just like them, the Defender was
supposed to be one of those crazy hoax stories.
Once in a while a newspaper would run a headline like BRITAIN'S VERY OWN SUPERHERO! next to
some photograph of the Defender that was so
blurry it didn't prove anything. But here he was—
the very same knight in white armor, right here,
right now.

Rather than wait for its master to dismount, the
horse collapsed in on itself, disappearing in an
instant into the Defender's spurs as easily as a
foldaway bicycle. The Black Lizard charged at him,
claws bared, but the Defender merely raised his
arm and a shimmering shield unfurled from his
wrist, parrying the blows. Advancing, he pulled out
a glowing sword and swung it at his opponent in
one smooth movement. The startled lizard dodged
the strike, but too late. A glancing blow to its
shoulder sent it spinning into the Tower wall with
all the impact of a car crash.

One of its black scales, severed by the Defender's strike, flew through the air and landed on the blanket covering Hayley's gran's lap. Hayley picked it up. It was almost too hot to hold. The sound of sirens wailed across the courtyard. Blue lights flashed through the archway. The Defender turned to look. It was all the chance the Black Lizard needed. It hauled itself out of the rubble, scuttled up one of the outer walls of the Tower, as fast and agile as a gecko, and disappeared over the top.

The Defender marched over to the lifeless body of the chief yeoman warder. Hayley and her gran watched in solemn silence as he knelt by the beefeater, head bowed as if in prayer. He spoke, his voice low but firm:

"May you never die a yeoman warder."

The Defender stood. His spurs glowed, and in a flash the ghostly horse unfurled itself between his legs, shook its mane, and lifted him silently into the night sky and away. No one spoke; no one moved.

Her gran smiled weakly. "See, Hales—told you it would be worth it."

Hayley looked down at the black scale in her hand and, without thinking, slipped it into her backpack.

-THREE-

The Heir and the Spare

What would it be this time? Detention? Suspension? Expulsion?

I wish, thought Alfie, as he inched his way out of bed and planted his feet on the cold floor. It wouldn't be good publicity for the world-famous Harrow School to throw out the heir to the throne. Besides, it wasn't the punishment he was worried about. It was the reaction of the world outside—what would they say about the latest gaffe from the accident-prone prince? All the attention he received still didn't make sense to Alfie. Weren't there more important things for people to talk about? Wars, natural disasters, terrible crimes, even last night's football scores. Did anyone really care that one boy got caught bunking off to eat pizza? Maybe this time would be different. Maybe the whole thing would have blown over by now.

He grabbed his towel, opened his bedroom door, and promptly put his foot in a trash can. At first Alfie thought his eyes must be playing tricks on him. But, no, there they were—big ones, small ones, shiny tin ones, dusty old wicker ones, gray plastic ones. Every single dustbin, wastepaper basket, and rubbish receptacle in the entire school was piled up in the hallway outside his room.

Laughter exploded from the staircase above. Alfie didn't need to look up to know that every other boy in the house was there, watching him as he stumbled through their oh-so-amusing trash can minefield.

Alfie tried to grin and bear it. "All right, very funny."

But now newspapers fluttered down all around him, like a blizzard of giant snowflakes. Plastered across every one of them was the image of Alfie's startled face staring up from his smelly hiding place the night before, each bearing a different, shrieking headline: RUBBISH PRINCE; TIME TO BIN THE ROYALS?, and his personal favorite, HIS TRASH-ESTY!

So much for it all blowing over.

It had been this way ever since Alfie first arrived at Harrow School on that blustery September morning six months ago. He'd tried his best to keep his head down and blend into the background. But Alfie soon learned that having HRH (His Royal Highness) in front of your name is like having a big bright spotlight trained on you 24/7. Yes, there were much worse positions he could have been born into—he was lucky that he would never be poor or hungry, and he knew it. But he had come to realize there was something else he would never be either: free.

Most people could go about their day without anyone paying them that much attention. Alfie couldn't enter a room without everyone looking at him. He couldn't walk down the street without people pointing and whispering to each other, or worse, shouting something or even chasing him. When most boys his age made a mistake or did something embarrassing—which, let's face it, is kind of the point of being a kid—they might wind up getting a lecture from their parents or made fun of by their friends. When Alfie messed up, his picture, along with a full rundown of every excruciating detail, was seen around the world within minutes.

Alfie couldn't understand why anybody would actually *want* to be famous. Every celebrity he'd ever met, usually at the boring palace receptions he was forced to go along to, seemed thoroughly miserable underneath all the glitz and glamour. He suspected that, like him, most would love to just flip a switch and turn off the attention. To go for a walk by themselves, buy a pizza, sit on a park bench and watch the world go by, rather than having the world watching them the whole time. Alfie would give anything just to be like everyone else—the unfairness of it made him angry if he thought about it for too long. But mainly it just made him nervous. Nervous of saying anything in case he said the wrong thing, nervous of trying anything new in case he made a fool of himself, nervous of—

"OI! PRINCESS!"

Oh, yeah, nervous of thugs like Mortimer. Alfie's least favorite person in the world, Sebastian Mortimer, had been six feet tall since he was eleven, and that was without including the impressive quiff of thick blond hair that rose from his head like a vanilla tidal wave. Alfie didn't know what he'd done to earn Mortimer's hatred. But he'd called Alfie "Princess" since their first day at school, always following it up with a laugh that was surprisingly high-pitched for such a gigantic meathead.

Most of the boys were happy to target Alfie with mere name-calling, pranks, and petty acts of teasing. Mortimer's brain worked on a rather more basic—some would say animal—level. Punching, twisting, squeezing, and pounding were more his style.

Alfie smiled, as if it might somehow defuse the situation. "Don't suppose we could skip the pummeling this morning, Mortimer? Bit of a rough night."

By way of an answer, Mortimer picked up one of the metal trash cans and heaved it in Alfie's direction. Alfie ducked just in time and it missed scalping him by inches. He looked around for help—where was Brian when he needed him? Ironically, Alfie was supposed to be safe inside the school grounds, so Brian kept a more discreet distance, only checking in on him a few times a day, not shadowing him like he did on the outside. *Some bodyguard he is*, thought Alfie as he dived to avoid a high-velocity dustbin lid hurled from Mortimer's grip like a discus.

"What's wrong, Princess? I thought you liked hanging about with the smelly trash? Probably makes you feel at home."

Alfie knew that none of the other boys, still watching in wide-eyed silence from the staircase, were likely to risk their necks for him. He was in trouble. His mind rattled through his options. He could fight back. Nah, that would just give Mortimer more of an excuse to hurt him. He could run. But Mortimer was bound to catch him. Maybe it was best just to stay where he was and take the beating. At least it would buy him a few days in the school clinic playing video games and eating ice cream and generally forgetting about who he was for a while. He closed his eyes and waited for Mortimer's fist to connect with his chin.

But the blow never came. When Alfie looked up, he was surprised to see the thug's arm being held back by a firm hand.

"Lay off Alfie for a while, would you, Morty? There's a good chap."

It was Richard. *Prince* Richard, Alfie's brother. Richard was Alfie's twin, but they were nonidentical, so you wouldn't know it. Except, of course, that everyone *did* know it—everyone in the world. It was a running gag that had followed Alfie around his entire life, because although Richard and he had been born a mere ten seconds apart, they couldn't have been less like each other. Alfie wasn't bad-looking, but he was clumsy: His arms and legs always seemed to be getting tangled up together; his hair never pointed in the same direction from one minute to the next; his clothes looked like they were trying to escape him and find someone less likely to spill ketchup down them. Richard was in a different league altogether.

"Get off me!" Mortimer was squirming under Richard's grip, but no matter which way he twisted, he couldn't find a way out.

I'm not surprised, thought Alfie. Richard was strong. In fact, he was taller, broader, sportier, smarter—just everything-*er* than Alfie. Whereas Alfie radiated shy awkwardness, Richard was one of those people who just seemed to glow with an inner confidence that couldn't be faked. Alfie had a theory about why this was—it was those ridiculous, annoying, stupid ten seconds! The difference between being the heir, like Alfie, or the "spare," as some called Richard. Not that his brother minded the nickname. There was no way Richard wanted to swap places. When you're first in line to the throne, everyone expects so much of you—you're supposed to be responsible, serious, clever—all the things Alfie struggled with big-time. But if you were second in line, like Richard, there was none of that. Sure, you still had the photographers following you sometimes, but it was nothing compared with the pressure heaped on the heir—on Alfie.

There was no doubt who everyone thought would make the better king one day—who *should* be the heir (clue: his name began with *R* and ended in *ichard*). The papers never failed to remind Alfie of this every time they wrote another piece about the hapless prince's latest misadventure. Richard just had *it*, and Alfie didn't, and that was the way it was.

Richard let go of Mortimer and shoved him away. The bully had enough sense not to push his luck.

"Whatever. Lucky for you, Princess." Mortimer kicked a trash can across the hall and slouched off. Sensing the show was over, the other boys dispersed.

Richard pulled Alfie to his feet and plucked a brown banana skin off his shoulder. "Interesting new aftershave you've got there, Alfie. You in one piece?"

"Yeah. Thanks, Richie."

Richard flashed a smile and patted him on the shoulder. Some brothers would have loved the opportunity to rub it in, but not Richard. He was too grown up for that. Sometimes Alfie couldn't believe they were related at all, let alone twins.

"*Illegitimi non carborundum*, brother!"

"Sorry, Rich, I don't speak . . . what is that?"

"Latin, Alf. Don't let the losers get you down. Something like that, anyway. I'm going for a run. See you at lunch?"

Alfie nodded, his humiliation complete. Saved by his little brother. Again. Richard strode off, casually tossing the banana skin over his shoulder and into a trash can without looking.

• • •

Back in his room after a hurried breakfast, Alfie sat at his computer and checked the time. He needed to write an overdue essay—the one he'd meant to start last night, before he decided he required some brain food first and went off on his ill-fated excursion.

Ring-ring.

A Skype call. His little sister, Princess Eleanor. She could see he was online; he couldn't exactly ignore her. Besides, she might need something. He pressed ANSWER. The image of his twelve-year-old sister—all freckles and rosy cheeks and hair nearly as crazy as his—popped up. She was grinning. "A trash can? Really?"

"It seemed like a good idea at the time. Listen, Ellie, I'm on a deadline, so—"

"Should have stayed in last night, then, shouldn't you?"

"Fair enough. How's school?"

Ellie was at an all-girls boarding school, on the south coast. Alfie had the feeling that she wasn't having a great time there, but his sister would never admit it. She might be small, but she'd always been tough. She loved to ride horses during the holidays, and Alfie had lost count of the number of times he'd seen her fall while attempting a jump that was too big. But she'd never cried. Not once. Even when she fractured her wrist.

"School's school. You know. So has Dad shouted at you yet?"

"Nope, but I'm sure he'll get around to it soon."

"He doesn't mean it, Alfie. He's just trying to help you."

Alfie smiled, but didn't answer. Ellie still idolized their dad, King Henry, and he didn't want to start an argument. Maybe it was a father-daughter thing. But to Alfie his dad was just one more person who liked to tell him what he already knew—that he wasn't good enough. He'd given up trying to please his father a long time ago.

Ellie could see Alfie didn't want to talk about it, so she changed tack.

"Hey, did you watch that clip I sent you?"

His sister was always sending him funny videos— not your average cute cat and baby clips either—but bizarre sketches from obscure American vloggers and Korean hidden-camera shows.

"The one about the zombies invading the all-night supermarket?" he asked.

Ellie rolled her eyes at him. "No! The one I sent this morning. Don't you ever check your inbox?"

"Not really. I'm not supposed to even use it. Too easy to hack into, apparently."

"Sucks to be you, Alf. Anyway, you should check it out—someone started taking it down as soon as it was posted, but I was too quick for them; I'd already saved it."

After they'd said good-bye, Alfie's hand hovered over the attachment Ellie had emailed him. He really needed to get started on his essay, but one quick video wouldn't hurt. Eyeing the clock nervously, he clicked open the file. A video started up. It claimed to be footage taken at the Tower of

London the night before and at first seemed to contain nothing but slightly out-of-focus tourists running around panicking. But then he saw the Black Lizard battering the soldiers into retreating, and moments later the Defender arriving to join the fight.

Alfie had seen photos of the supposed British superhero before, of course—everyone had. There were vintage black-and-white images of him astride a shimmering silver horse, carrying a battle-scarred Spitfire down to an airfield, distant videos of him propping up a badly listing cruise liner, or shielding Christmas shoppers from a car bomb. But nothing at quite such close quarters as this.

The rest of the Tower footage was very shaky and handheld. *Probably to hide the special effects,* thought Alfie. He'd always assumed that the reports about the "white knight superhero" were hoaxes, but someone must have gone to a lot of effort to pull this off. *Amazing what some people will do with their weekends,* he mused as the video played out. Right at the end, something odd caught his attention—a piece of the lizard man's skin seemed to be sliced off and fly toward the camera, only to land in the lap of an old lady in a wheelchair. The teenage girl next to her picked it up. She looked genuinely scared, not like she was acting at all.

RRRRRRRING!

The bell for first period startled Alfie out of his daydream. He slammed his laptop shut, annoyed with himself. He was out of time.

- FOUR -

The Keeper of the Scale

Hayley had never been a very good liar. Honesty ran in the family. One of her gran's several million sayings was "honesty is the first chapter in the book of wisdom," and her mum, who used to run an electrical repair business when she was alive, was forever saying "honesty is the best policy." So when Hayley found herself on the phone to her school that morning, about to pretend she was sick and couldn't come in, she messed it all up.

"Good morning, Rook's Heath School, Claire speaking. How can I help?" The school secretary sounded hassled.

"Hi, it's Hayley Hicks. Grade nine. I can't come in today . . ." Hayley stopped talking abruptly and squeezed her eyes shut, ready to fake a coughing fit. Big mistake. She'd found out last night, while trying (and failing) to sleep, that closing her eyes was like pressing PLAY on the most insane film montage you'd ever seen. Knights on spectral horses. Tourists yelling and running everywhere.

Lizard men with red eyes climbing up the walls of the Tower of London.

"Why can't you come in? Hello?" The school secretary's voice was high-pitched in Hayley's ear, snapping her out of it.

How could anyone even think of doing anything today other than trying to deal with the most earth-shattering event in the history of mankind ever?

"The Defender is real! Haven't you even seen the news?!" Hayley shouted, then hung up. Oops.

Superheroes, monsters, magic—it's all actually true! The idea was frightening, mad, and exciting all at the same time. It was like someone had ripped off the roof of the world and pumped in pure, undiluted wonder.

But when Hayley padded into the living room and switched on the TV, all the news was showing was a boring report about fishing quotas in the North Sea. Then there was a story about gasoline prices (going up), followed by the weather (rain on the way). Flabbergasted, Hayley flicked through the rest of the channels, but there was nothing. Where were the headlines? LIZARD MONSTER ATTACKS TOWER OF LONDON or maybe KNIGHT ON FLYING HORSE SAVES THE DAY! Hayley didn't understand. It was like everyone in charge had taken a vow of silence about it.

Hayley went back to her room and fired up her

old laptop, searching online instead. What the world *was* talking about endlessly was how Prince Alfred had run away from his posh school and been photographed in a trash can. Hayley couldn't believe Britain still had a royal family (*in the twenty-first century? Seriously?*), not that she would ever dream of saying so to her gran. But what did Prince Alfie have to run away from, anyway? He was rich and lived in a palace with a hundred rooms. Hayley and her gran shared a two-bedroom public-housing apartment and practically lived off potatoes (if you ever needed creative tips on a thousand and one ways to cook a spud, Hayley was your girl). They were lucky they still had the lights on—the electricity company was threatening to cut them off because they were behind on paying the bills again.

Tying her hair back to stop it from distracting her, Hayley went into deep-search mode, scouring chat rooms dedicated to Defender sightings. Her heart leapt when she found a video link to TOWER OF LONDON: NEW DEFENDER SIGHTING! But when she clicked on it, the link was dead.

Someone had written, *They don't want us to know. They've deleted it. They want to shut us down! #Defender #Truth* in reply below. But directly below that, someone else had added, *You all have such great imaginations. But news flash: Superheroes and monsters don't exist!*

Yes, they do! thought Hayley, *and I can prove it . . .*

Hayley crossed the bedroom to her wardrobe and lifted out her backpack. She unzipped a small pocket and pulled out the Black Lizard's scale. It had been hot when she grabbed it at the Tower, and even though it had cooled, there was still something about it that made her wary. She held the scale by its edges, turning it over in the light. Etched into its smooth black surface were tattoo-like swirls that wrapped around each other. If you stared at them long enough, they formed into the shape of snakes, their eyes flashing and fangs bared.

She wanted to call it beautiful, but there was something else, some kind of power deep within it, humming away. It felt alive in the same way you knew a TV was on even when it was on standby. And it felt wrong. It felt . . . evil.

Hayley shivered. The thing that had really kept her up all night was the memory of the old beef-eater lying broken in the dirt, whispering his last words to her . . . "God save the king." She couldn't forget that the scale she was holding in her hands came from the hideous creature that had killed him.

Ping!

Hayley jumped as her phone rattled and a text message from her gran popped up: *Tea!!!!* Hayley had reprogrammed an old phone to piggyback off her network for free. It had taken her gran a few weeks to master texting, but now that she'd cracked it, the requests for tea, the TV remote control, and updates about what was for dinner (baked potatoes, usually) were nonstop. Hayley sighed. Superheroes or no superheroes, her gran still needed looking after. Hayley zipped the scale away, buried the backpack in her wardrobe, and switched back into caregiver mode.

Hayley looked in as she passed by the living room. "You could say please, Gran!"

Her gran was watching a daytime quiz show and shouting at one of the contestants. "The answer's Moscow! I didn't think they made people's brains so small."

At least her memory was up to scratch this morning, which meant she was having one of her good days. After Hayley's mum had died, her gran had become her guardian. But over the last couple of years, they had swapped roles. Hayley didn't mind—she didn't have time to, what with all the cooking, cleaning, fetching her gran's pension, carefully logging which medicines she'd taken on a spreadsheet she'd created, oh, and going to school. She'd even rigged up emergency red cords in every room, which her gran could pull if she was in trouble and which sent an alert straight to Hayley's phone. There had been a few false alarms, of course, when Hayley had rushed home, only to discover that her gran had gotten muddled up trying to close the bedroom curtains. But it was worth it to know she was safe.

Hayley never told anyone about everything she did for her gran—Hayley didn't do whining. But it did have its downsides. She couldn't invite friends back to the apartment anymore in case her gran had a funny turn. Boyfriends were a nonstarter. She'd even had to say no to joining the school's athletics team—Hayley was the fastest sprinter by far, but practices were twice a week after school and she just couldn't risk being away for that long. Her sports teacher had accused her of being lazy, but she just bit her lip and said nothing. It didn't matter what people thought. Her gran had looked after her when she needed someone and now she was going to do the same. End of discussion.

"It's Admiral Lord Nelson, you fool!" her gran shouted at the TV. "What do they teach you kids in school these days, eh?"

Hayley was pleased that her gran didn't seem too shaken by what had happened at the Tower last night. In fact, she had taken great pleasure in giving a blow-by-blow account to some of the neighbors in the tower-block elevator when they'd finally made it back home: how they'd visited the

Crown Jewels and had lunch in the café; how Hayley had gotten them tickets to see the Ceremony of the Keys; how a knight and a lizard had a big fight in front of them, before the knight flew away on his horse. She'd said it as casually as if she were talking about a delayed train. But Hayley could read the neighbors' minds: *Poor old Mrs. Hicks—she really is losing it.*

As Hayley made the tea, her gran shuffled in with her walker and started to rifle through the post on the kitchen table.

"What are you looking for, Gran?"

"Tsch, that useless shop, they've forgotten to deliver Lawrence's newspaper—again!"

Hayley winced. Lawrence was her grandfather, but he'd died twenty years before. Sometimes her gran would hold entire conversations with the empty chair in the living room, thinking her husband was still there.

"All right, I'll call them," said Hayley as she helped her gran back into the living room. "Come and have your tea."

• • •

Outside, a gray car with tinted windows pulled up opposite the tower block. The woman at the wheel looked far too tall to be comfortable in any car, let alone this standard-issue undercover pile of junk.

Her seat was pushed back so far that any rear passengers would have found themselves crushed. Her name was Fulcher. She was as ugly as she was mean. And she was very, very mean—when the job called for it. Her immense shoulders reached all the way across to the passenger seat and the much smaller frame of her partner, a neat, cold-eyed man called Turpin. Fulcher and Turpin had accepted long ago that they did not like each other. They never talked for fun. But they also knew that together they made an effective team, and the exceedingly secretive arm of the government that employed them prized results above all else.

"What now?" grunted Fulcher, tearing open a packet of the strongest breath mints that science had ever produced. In the early days, Turpin had told her that bad breath was the least of her problems. She had cracked three of his teeth for that one, and he'd never again made the mistake of assuming his colleague had a sense of humor.

"Now," replied Turpin, focusing his high-powered binoculars on Hayley's fourteenth-floor apartment, "we wait."

- FIVE -

The Chain of Destiny

"We need a leader!"

Alfie's history class was standing in the middle of the cricket pitch. Their teacher, Professor Lock, was striding up and down in front of them, carrying a metal detector. He fixed Alfie with his piercing blue eyes and smiled.

"How about you, Alfie?"

Alfie shook his head and looked at his feet. Mortimer shoulder-bumped him out of the way and grabbed the metal detector for himself. "I'll do it."

"Very well, Sebastian. Eager to learn as ever, I see," said Lock. "Switch it on and get sweeping— head for the pavilion."

With a cocky grin, Mortimer thumped the ON button and started to swing the metal detector back and forth. The class fell in behind Professor Lock as he strolled across the immaculate grass.

Cameron Lock was like no other teacher Alfie had ever known. Harrow School's youngest ever head of history, Lock had arrived a year ago following a research career that had produced a couple of books few had heard of and little else. Still, he'd beaten several older, more qualified applicants to the post, and it was soon clear why. In teaching he had found his calling.

"Sebastian, what do you want to be when you escape this place?" asked Professor Lock.

"Investment banker," snapped back Mortimer, without hesitation.

"The perfect job for someone like you," Lock said. Mortimer's smile was uncertain. That was the other thing about Lock—it was impossible sometimes to know if he was joking or not.

"Jamie, what about you?"

A bright-eyed boy at the front answered, "Surgeon, sir."

Lock nodded. "An admirable ambition . . . Tony?"

"Superhero crime fighter, sir!" piped up the tiny Chinese boy with the red glasses behind Alfie. The boys laughed and he took a bow. Tony was a serious eccentric; he never seemed to care what other people thought of him, which is why Alfie liked him.

"Maybe a little too ambitious, Tony. But you never know. Not too fast, Sebastian, you don't want to miss anything!"

Mortimer scowled and swept the metal detector extra slowly.

"And, Alfie, what does your future hold?"

Alfie felt the eyes of the class shoot his way as he opened his mouth, struggling for a meaningful answer. Was Lock really asking *him*? What did he expect him to say? The other boys snickered as Alfie closed his mouth again, his face getting redder by the second. He was saved by a sudden *beep-beep-beep* coming from the metal detector.

"Found something!" yelled Mortimer. The class stopped and gathered around him, excited.

Lock eased his way to the front. "If history tells us anything, it's that we never truly know what's coming next." He pulled out a small gardening trowel and tossed it to the ground at Mortimer's feet. "Well, dig it up, then!"

The boys looked at one another, shocked. "But . . . it's the cricket pitch, sir," said Mortimer.

"So what? You have to dig if you want the treasure!"

Mortimer shrugged, knelt down, and plunged the trowel into the soft turf. He pulled out a clod of earth and shook it until it landed upside down, revealing something shiny stuck in the soil. A small silver coin. Lock picked it out, brushed it clean, and held it up for the class to see. It was thin, with rough, uneven edges. On one side was the crude image of a man's face in profile, wearing some kind of band around his head; on the other, some strange symbols Alfie didn't recognize.

"This is a penny from the reign of King Alfred the Great, over a thousand years ago—ruler of Wessex and, some say, first true king of England."

"What was so great about him?" sneered Mortimer.

"Well, he saved the country from the Vikings for starters," replied Professor Lock, "not to mention created the first proper education and legal systems. But here's the interesting part—he was never supposed to be king. Alfred was the youngest of five brothers. It's kind of amazing that we've even heard of him . . . Keep searching, Seb."

Mortimer groaned and turned the metal detector back on. He'd taken only a few more steps when the machine beeped again. It was another coin. This one had a Latin inscription around the edges and bore the image of a noble-looking woman wearing a crown and a ruff around her neck.

"Elizabeth the First," declared Professor Lock.

"Wow!" blurted Jamie.

"He planted it here, you moron," hissed Mortimer.

Lock smiled and passed the coin around. "No one wanted her to be queen. Declared illegitimate by her own father, imprisoned by her own half-sister. Yet she survived, took the throne, and ruled for nearly fifty years, successfully defeating the invading Spanish Armada and becoming one of our finest ever monarchs."

The metal detector beeped once more. Mortimer stooped and came up holding a dirty, but new, two-pound coin, bearing the face of Alfie's father, the current king.

Lock looked at it, amused. "Now this one was nothing to do with me," said the teacher. "King Henry the Ninth. These days, of course, the monarch is more of a figurehead; they don't exercise any real power."

"Guess royals aren't what they used to be," sniped Mortimer at Alfie.

"Tell you what, Sebastian," said Lock, taking the metal detector and stamping the loose clods of earth back into the pitch. "For being such an excellent treasure-seeker, you get to keep any one of the coins—your choice."

Mortimer snatched back the two-pound coin. "I'll take the one I can spend," he said smugly.

Lock winced. "Should have gone for the one you could sell," he said, flipping the ancient King Alfred penny in the air and pocketing it. "Not sure banking's really for you, matey."

The class laughed. Mortimer scowled and muttered something about history being a "stupid waste of time anyway."

Suddenly an indignant "Oi!" drifted their way from the far side of the pitch. The head groundsman had spotted them and he did not look happy. Lock waved at him and hurried the boys back toward the school.

As they reached the safety of the history department, Professor Lock pulled Alfie aside. "Can I have a word?"

"If it's about the essay, I'm sorry it's late, sir," said Alfie. "I'll get it in tomorrow, though, I promise."

Lock waved a hand dismissively. "That? I'd forgotten all about it. Let's pretend you didn't mention it, eh? No, I just wanted to say sorry. I didn't mean to embarrass you out there with all that monarchy business. I know it must be awkward for you."

"Kind of hard to avoid in history, I suppose, sir."

Lock laughed. "Good lad. Listen, I think I get your problem."

"My problem?"

"Your motivation problem. It must be tough to care about the future when your fate has been decided for you since the day you were born."

Alfie was speechless. It was as if Lock had reached into the darkest corner of his mind and shone a light on the thing he'd been secretly feeling his whole life. That strange empty sensation, deep down in his gut: that feeling of total and utter pointlessness. Like nothing he did mattered. He tried not to think of the future, because when he did, all he saw was more of the same—a life not his own,

governed by stupid rules and traditions and ceremonies he neither understood nor cared about.
His father's life. The life that would one day be
his. He'd always tried to put it as far from his conscious thoughts as he could, and yet he had never
realized how much it stopped him from living in
the here and now. Not until Professor Lock said
those words to him and brought it all crashing into
focus.

Lock smiled, sympathetic, and pointed up at
the grand portrait of Winston Churchill, Britain's
greatest prime minister, who had led them to
victory during the Second World War, and—as
the headmaster never tired of mentioning in
assembly—a former pupil at their school. Another
legend that felt impossible for Alfie to live up to.

"He hated it here, you know," said Professor
Lock. "Barely scraped through his exams, didn't
have any friends. No one expected much of young
Winston."

Alfie was amazed. "But he was . . . he was
Churchill."

"Ha, yes, he was, eventually. But you know what
made him great? He was never afraid to do his own
thing, strike out and find his own path. Even when
people said he shouldn't. Do you know what he
said about fate?" Lock put his hands on his hips and

barked out in his best gruff Churchill impression: "It is a mistake to try to look too far ahead. The chain of destiny can only be grasped one link at a time."

As Alfie walked to his next lesson, his feet felt like they were skating across the hallway floor, disconnected from the rest of his body. Lock's words had lit a fire under him. He was sick of people telling him what to do. He decided there and then, he was going to do what *he* wanted for a change. From now on, he was going to choose his own direction.

"WALES!"

A bony hand landed on his shoulder and spun him around. It was the deputy headmaster, Mr. Beakley, a pig-eyed, cruel little man, who had one level to his voice, and that was "shouty." He loved to use Alfie's "official" surname. It was so stupid. Who else was named after a country?

"Headmaster's study. Now, Wales!"

Alfie hesitated. He wanted to yell back at Beakley, scream at the top of his lungs and tell him just where he could stick his rules and his orders.

"Coming, sir." Alfie turned and followed Beakley down the hall, head bowed. All the air had gone out of him like a deflated balloon.

Alfie reached the enormous oak door to the headmaster's study, adjusted his tie, and took a breath. He would listen, nod, say sorry about the whole pizza adventure, and that would be that. No problem. He'd been hauled in front of the headmaster before and no doubt would be again. But when Mr. Beakley opened the door, it took Alfie less than two seconds to realize that a) he wasn't about to get a telling-off from the headmaster (it was much, much worse than that), and b) that he had been, appropriately enough, royally stitched up.

"Hello, Alfred."

Only one man could imbue those two simple words with a lifetime of disapproval and disappointment.

"Hello, Father."

King Henry the Ninth sat straight-backed behind the grand leather-topped desk, in the chair that Alfie doubted the headmaster had ever let anyone else sit in. His father's beard was even grayer than last time Alfie had seen him, back in the Christmas holidays. His face was lined with worry, his shoulders tense.

Behind the king lurked the lofty, skeletal figure of his chief advisor, the Lord Chamberlain. He'd been there, a permanent fixture in his dad's shadow for as long as Alfie could remember. Dress rules for the palace staff had relaxed a great deal over the years, but the Lord Chamberlain was seriously old school and always wore a dark formal suit with long tails, breeches, and black shoes with silver buckles. It was impossible to say how old he was, but if Alfie had to hazard a guess, he would have said about two hundred.

"All right, LC?"

Nothing annoyed the old retainer more than using his nickname, which is precisely why Alfie did it. Besides, he had no idea what the Lord Chamberlain's real name was, or even if he had one. The old man nodded the smallest of nods at Alfie and hissed a curt, "Your Highness." But the arched eyebrow and curl to the upper lip betrayed what the old geezer really thought of him.

A low growl issued from under the desk as a long black nose poked out, sniffing. *Oh great*, thought Alfie, *Dad's brought the killer pooch too.*

"Settle down, Herne!" huffed the king.

The huge, steely-haired Irish wolfhound withdrew and wrapped its body around its master's feet. Herne had always hated Alfie—the dog had once chased him around the palace gardens and up a tree, where he'd had to wait for the whole afternoon until Brian came to the rescue.

"Well?"

Apparently his father expected him to say something. The front pages of the newspapers were spread across the desk between them, all featuring photographs of Alfie in the trash. "All I wanted was a pizza. You should taste the food in here—it's revolting."

The king emitted a deep sigh and rubbed his neck until a red patch started to appear under the skin. *He looks so tired*, thought Alfie.

"I can't keep defending you, Alfie. You're not a child anymore."

"Well, technically I am. For a couple more years anyway."

When it came to judging the right moment to crack a joke, Alfie scored a D every time. The Lord Chamberlain cast his nose to the ceiling, as if a nasty smell had just offended him.

The steel returned to the king's gaze. "You know what is expected of you, Alfie. All I'm asking is that you stay out of trouble. I don't have time to deal with this nonsense."

"Why not?" Alfie said it almost as soon as he'd thought it.

His father's neck was growing redder. "Pardon?"

Alfie persisted. It was going badly anyway, so why self-edit now? "I mean, I know you have the royal visits and dinners and ceremonies and all that, but, well, it's not exactly life and death, is it?"

The Lord Chamberlain's face had become so pinched, it looked like he might implode.

"I just don't see why you're so stressed all the time," continued Alfie. "I mean, it's only for show, isn't it? Wave at the crowds, cut a ribbon here, smash a bottle on a ship there. It's not like our family really has to *do* anything, is it?"

"Oh, for goodness' sake, Alfie. We've talked about this before. What is it that you want?"

"I don't know. To do what everyone else does. To go for a walk without a bodyguard. To make friends without worrying whether I can trust them or not. Maybe get an ordinary job one day. Just to be, you know, normal. Not some kind of . . . useless freak from a history book."

King Henry pounded a clenched fist on the desk. Herne whimpered beneath it. Alfie had gone too far. That much was clear. But he'd never seen his father so angry.

"YOU WILL *NOT* TALK ABOUT YOUR FAMILY THAT WAY! IF YOU ONLY KNEW WHAT WE'D DONE FOR THIS COUNTRY—"

Alfie was spared the rest of the lecture by the ringing of the phone on the headmaster's desk. The Lord Chamberlain picked it up, listened, and replaced the receiver without saying anything. He whispered in the king's ear before moving to the study door and holding it open. King Henry looked away from his son, his thoughts suddenly lost somewhere else. His face resumed the blank, resigned look that Alfie had seen so many times before.

The king gathered up Herne's lead and stepped past Alfie to the door. "I'm afraid there's something I must attend to at once."

Alfie tried to hold his tongue, but he couldn't. "There's always something more important, isn't there? More important than your family."

His father froze in the doorway, his back to Alfie. Herne growled once more, but Alfie ignored him. He was too angry to be scared. For a moment Alfie thought his father would turn on him, shout or scream—he yearned for him to do it, anything to show that he cared.

But the king didn't turn. He just moved off to whatever duty lay beyond, leaving Alfie alone, anger still burning in his throat.

SIX

Death Among
the Stones

Wyvern's hooves carved through thin clouds, scattering them into droplets, as the ghostly horse carried her master across the night sky. Several miles to the north, the Defender could make out the winking lights of an airliner heading toward the sea. Thousands of feet below, the countryside was laid out like patchwork, the lights of villages and towns shining like clusters of gold coins. Wyvern banked to the right, giving her rider a clear view of their destination as it came into view.

Stonehenge.

The Defender's great helmet pivoted slowly, scanning from the tall trilithon slabs, huddled together like unruly teeth in the jaws of a long-dead giant, to the burial mounds that dotted around them. These were the resting places of the men who had dragged these rocks two hundred miles from a Welsh quarry to this barren plain. The land around here was known to be special long before some ancient tribe decided to heave this crude monument into existence. The invisible lines of power that converged deep beneath the earth had always attracted powerful men, both good and bad—to rally their followers, to seek divine approval, to be interred in the sacred soil for eternity. Tonight was no different. Once more, Stonehenge would play host to events that would shape the future of the kingdom.

Because something else was lurking here tonight. He could see the telltale signs of it now— an ugly, dark scar in the middle of the stone circle, the spoil heap of a recent excavation. Was this the work of the creature he had first encountered at the Tower? Was it searching for something under the great stones?

A twitch on the reins and Wyvern responded, tucking her legs close into her ethereal body and plunging them both into a steep, soundless dive.

They leveled out a clear mile from Stonehenge, only a few feet above the ground. Woods, lanes, and hedgerows streaked past—it wasn't much cover, but it would have to do. Surprise would be the key; his enemy had been lucky to escape before. This time would be different.

Then he saw it. The hulking shape of the Black Lizard emerging from the crater it had dug, scales caked in mud, back turned. Keeping one glove on

Wyvern's reins, the Defender unsheathed his sword and pointed it at his onrushing target; he was going to run this foul monster through.

The Defender kicked his spurs and Wyvern responded, finding more impossible speed—close, so close, just the single road that cut through the valley to clear now. He braced for impact, his sword aimed at the center of the Black Lizard's back.

BEEEEEEEEP!

They had leapt the road right in front of a huge articulated truck, which slammed on its brakes and jackknifed with a hideous screech of tires. The Black Lizard turned, the Defender's sword inches from its back, and sidestepped. Its attackers flew clean past. Wyvern disappeared into her master's spurs as he crashed into one of the giant stones, breaking it in two.

Stunned, the Defender looked up to see the monster standing over him, red eyes burning in the night, slime dripping from its long jaws. A tail unfurled from behind the creature, thick and studded with vicious spikes—a tail that he could swear had not been there the first time they had met. The Defender rolled clear as it came whipping down at him, spikes burying themselves into the ground. The Black Lizard roared and heaved its tail up again, swiping at the Defender's side. He had just enough time to summon a shield from his arm bracelet, but the impact still sent him hurtling through the air.

The Defender was reeling. It wasn't just his opponent's new tail, or increased strength, or improved speed—although those were startling enough. There was something else. He could feel it in the air. Power crackled off his enemy like electricity. Something had changed since their encounter at the Tower.

The dark nightmare came at him again. Relentless, swiping with its dagger claws, pushing one of the great stones over with fearsome strength. The Defender dodged as four tons of carved rock fell toward him, using the cover of the impact to launch his own counterstrike, surging too close for the Black Lizard's tail to be of any use. He swung his sword at his enemy's neck, but his opponent parried with a powerful arm, the shock wave from the clash rolling out like a thunderclap across the empty plain.

Last time he struck the beast with his sword, he had cut it, but now the creature's armor of scales was much harder. *How had this thing grown so much stronger so fast?*

Unable to hold his ground, the Defender backed off. A split second later, the lizard's tail struck his chest full force at point-blank range, sending him spinning onto his back. A mighty clawed hand gripped the Defender's sword arm, squeezing the weapon from his grasp.

The Black Lizard thumped its tail down at the Defender again. This time his shield met the strike, but the force of it sent him through the topsoil and into the gaping maw of the crater at the center of the stone circle. A second blow, a third, and the Defender's shield cracked in half, shards falling over his battered armor. The Black Lizard planted a heavy, clawed foot onto his chest, pushing him farther down into the hole. Pain coursed through the Defender's body. He could feel his armor failing.

Moving as fast as he dared, without making it too obvious what he was doing, the Defender pulled a hand from the soil, directing his shaking fist at the nearest fallen stone. The ring on his finger, a cross of rubies laid against a blue sapphire, glowed as he tried to calm his mind. The Black Lizard ground its heel farther into the Defender's chest. Fighting for breath, he knew he had to buy more time.

"What do you want?" he demanded.

"Power." The Black Lizard's voice was a dark hiss.

The Black Lizard reached inside its scaly armor and pulled out something small and golden, its edges jagged and broken, glinting from beneath a thick layer of mud. It seemed familiar to the Defender—like a distant memory, something from a dream, or a bedtime story his mother had once told him. Then he knew. *Could it be? Was it real?* And in that instant he understood what the Black Lizard was doing here in the middle of the night, digging in the earth.

"Now do you understand, knight?" The Black Lizard chuckled.

The Defender directed his mind to focus all his energy through the ring and toward the tall monolith of rock behind the Black Lizard. He had to stop this beast; he had to warn the others—it was his last chance. The huge stone rocked, stood upright once more, then lifted completely off the ground, rising high above the creature's head. Turning his fist upward, the Defender sent the great mass of rock crashing toward his foe.

But the lizard was too fast. Sensing danger at the last second, it stepped aside, and the immense stone speared into the earth. The Defender had missed.

The Black Lizard emitted a low, guttural laugh. The Defender slumped onto his back, fighting for breath, staring up at the indifferent stars. He closed his eyes, knowing this was the end. Others would have to take up the fight; his part was done. His cracked lips recited his knightly motto one final time.

"*Non ducor, duco . . .*"

The Black Lizard spun its heavy tail down at the white knight, burying its largest spike deep in the Defender's chest. The entire plain quaked under the impact. A quarter of a mile away the asphalt of the road cracked like glass, swallowing the wreck of the jackknifed truck, as trees groaned and splintered in the grip of the tremor. Around the two warriors, the last of the ancient stones toppled, until nothing was left standing except for the victorious dark monster itself.

The Black Lizard withdrew its tail from the Defender's chest with a sickening wet sound. Blood rose out from the wound and spread across the fallen warrior's chest plate. It seemed to glow blue for a moment, then darkened as it ran off into the mud. The Black Lizard stood, head bowed, almost as if it could not quite believe it had won this particular battle, almost as if it was sorry that it had.

The throbbing of rotor blades came from across the hills. A police helicopter's searchlight swept over the plain as it approached. With a final glance down at its victim, the Black Lizard stepped out of the crater and slipped away into the darkness.

The Defender lay quite still amid the wreckage of Stonehenge. At his feet, his spurs spun open and the shape of his horse grew beneath his lifeless body. Craning her neck to nuzzle her master, Wyvern whinnied. Then rising into the air, she carried him away, disappearing into the clouds just as the helicopter arrived over the battle-scarred field.

- SEVEN -

"Your Majesty"

A strange thought occurred to Alfie as he flew backward across the broad oak table, into a bookshelf. *I've never been punched in the face before.*

He'd had the odd scrap with his brother when they were growing up, of course (he always lost), and Mortimer was hardly gentle, but a full-blooded fist thrown in anger at the bridge of his nose? That was a new experience, and not one he wanted to repeat in a hurry. Harrow School's Vaughan Library was probably not the best place for his first public brawl either—but then, he hadn't come here looking for a fight.

Alfie had been trying to lie low all day. The school was buzzing with rumors: King Henry was heard shouting at his son (true); Alfie was being suspended (not true); King Henry had chased Alfie around the headmaster's office and spanked him (oh, *please*). The rest of the day had been a write-off; how could you pay attention to lessons when everyone was snickering behind your back? All he wanted to do was crawl into a deep hole and never come out, and the closest thing he could find to that was the school library.

"Prince AWOL! Thought we'd agreed, no more secret outings."

Alfie sighed and looked around. Brian was marching after him in the economical style the army had taught him years ago.

"It's all right, Brian. No more pizza runs for me. I'm going to the library." Alfie held up his schoolbag. "So you can be 'at ease,' or do whatever it is you guys do."

Brian made a show of scanning the area. "Hitting the books, eh? Shall I alert the newspapers? This is quite the event. Oh, and by the way, we say 'stand down.'" Brian walked off whistling as Alfie went inside.

The library was as quiet as he'd hoped it would be. There was only a scattering of other boys here: teenage book geeks, homesick overseas students, and anyone too weedy to play rugby. *Misfits one and all. I fit right in*, thought Alfie. He found a study desk tucked away in the far corner and settled down to work.

Despite the day he'd had, Alfie quickly became absorbed in one of the books from Professor Lock's reading list. It was all about his namesake, King Alfred the Great, and the Viking invasion that had swept down from Scandinavia and across Britain.

On Christmas Day, Alfred had been ambushed by the Vikings and forced into hiding with a small band of loyal men. They'd found an island in the middle of a marsh in the West Country and lived off the land before launching a counterattack. Alfie ran his fingers over a picture of King Alfred, an ancient woodcut that showed the bearded king sitting in a peasant's hovel, long hair unkempt, looking deep into a fire.

How weird that I'm related to you, thought Alfie. He was generations and generations down the line, but still descended from a man in a history book, linked together by an invisible, incalculably long cosmic rope. *You hid in a swamp. I'm lying low in a library—*

"Evening, Princess."

Mortimer was standing behind him, beaming with cruel pleasure. Alfie lurched to his feet, but Mortimer shoved him back down.

"Don't get up, Your Lordship."

Behind Mortimer, some of his sheeplike followers had also materialized and were giggling like their leader had just dropped the funniest joke bomb in the history of laughs. Alfie was surrounded. The panic-button-enabled cell phone was in his bag, out of reach. He was ashamed that he felt so scared. What kind of person needs a bodyguard to protect him from other kids, anyway?

Sensing something in Alfie's look, Mortimer smiled. "Oh dear, your brother not here to fight your battle for you?" One of Mortimer's goons wedged the library door shut with a fire extinguisher.

Images flickered through Alfie's mind of the next five minutes: his head in a toilet, being made to kiss a toilet brush; maybe they'd strip his clothes and leave him naked outside. Imagine the headlines *that* would make.

A sudden surge of anger rose up in him. He'd never gone out of his way to provoke this thug. *If I wasn't Prince of Wales, he wouldn't even know I existed.* He was sick of all the looks and whispers. He was tired of feeling so . . . so *powerless.* Alfie's fist clenched, and before he even knew what he was doing, he was cocking his arm back and unleashing a full-on punch, aimed straight at Mortimer's stupid nose. Everything slowed down. He even had a chance to savor the look of dumb alarm on Mortimer's face as his fist closed in and . . .

Swish. Missed. Mortimer sidestepped it easily.

Alfie stumbled over, the momentum of his unsuccessful punch unbalancing him. Mortimer's crew burst out laughing. Alfie was tempted to join in—it was the miss to end all misses. But Mortimer wasn't laughing, and his stare was pure evil. Which is why he thumped the heir to the throne of Great

Britain and Northern Ireland clean across the desk and into a bookshelf.

None of the library geeks were quick enough to catch the moment on their phones, but by the time Alfie had found his feet and launched his own rather clumsy rugby tackle at Mortimer's legs, a dozen recording devices were ready to capture it for posterity. The first video of the "unprovoked attack" by the Prince of Wales on an "innocent fellow pupil" would be online fewer than seven seconds later.

Alfie had picked himself up, but was backed against a wall, like a fox surrounded by a pack of hounds.

Mortimer towered over him. "You're pathetic, Princess." He looked at his friends. "And to think this loser is supposed to be king one day!"

"I don't want to be king," Alfie yelled. "I just want to be left alone!"

He lunged at Mortimer again, but as he did, a sudden, immense pain speared through his chest. He doubled over, crying out in agony. A wave of intense cold swept over him, as if his entire body had been plunged into ice. His limbs went rigid and he fell to the floor, shaking. His vision blurred—he couldn't see, couldn't think—there was nothing but the overwhelming sensation of stabbing pain.

The others looked at each other, confused.

"You expect us to fall for that? Get up," Mortimer scoffed.

Tony, the Chinese boy from Alfie's class, ran out from under the desk where he'd been hiding and went nose to nose with Mortimer—well, nose to belly button, anyway.

"Leave him alone! Can't you see he's hurt?"

Mortimer laughed and swatted Tony to the side. Alfie tried to say something—"Help me, I'm dying, heart attack"—but all that came out was a low moan. His skin was gray, his eyes rolling back in their sockets.

"Stand up, you wuss," Mortimer said, but even he sounded a little less sure now.

CRASH. The library door splintered open and the next thing Alfie knew, Mortimer was being lifted away from him and thrust against an appalled-looking marble bust of the school's founder.

Brian tightened his grip on Mortimer's collar and hissed into his ear. "Unless you want to spend the rest of the night inside a cell at the local prison, I suggest you leave. Now."

With that, Brian tossed Mortimer in the general direction of the door and turned his attention to Alfie, who was breathing easier but still in a daze. It was like he was seeing the world through somebody else's eyes; everything was out of focus, the colors intense.

Tony knelt down next to Brian. "He had some kind of fit. Is he all right?"

"He'll live." Brian wrapped an arm around Alfie's shoulders. "Can you stand? We need to go."

Brian held him up as they hurried out into the cold air. Every step Alfie took was an effort. Professor Lock appeared, walking past the library. He eyed the young prince, concerned. "Are you OK, Alfie?"

Alfie tried to lift his head to the friendly voice, but Brian was pushing him on, toward the playing fields. Where were they going? Alfie was just summoning up the strength to ask, when suddenly he thought he sensed something rushing toward him out of the dark: something immense and powerful, searching for him, homing in on him. But when he looked back, there was nothing there.

"Brian . . . ," Alfie croaked. "What's happening?" But the low *whump-whump-whump* of rotor blades cut through the night's air, blowing away his words. A helicopter was coming in to land, the downdraft whipping up a tornado of twigs and grass cuttings. Brian hauled Alfie into the chopper and moments later they were high in the air, the lights of Harrow disappearing far beneath them.

Alfie tried to speak again, his voice weak. "Where are we going?"

"The palace."

"Why?"

"It's your father . . ."

· · ·

Alfie didn't need Brian to help him when they landed in the gardens of Buckingham Palace. His strength had come back and he leapt off the chopper. He ran through the music room and up the grand staircase, taking the steps two at a time, ignoring the lingering pain in his chest. All he could think of was the last conversation he'd had with his father.

Inside the grand entrance hall, the household staff were up, despite the hour. Alfie was aware of them standing there, as if on parade, but his eyes were focused only on the stairs that led to his father's bedroom.

"Prince Alfred." The Lord Chamberlain's clipped voice. Alfie ignored it. There was no time tonight for that meddling old codger and his lectures on correct etiquette and protocol. He must see his dad.

"Alfie!"

Alfie stopped and turned back down the steps. It was Richard, still in his sports gear, dried mud on his knees and his face uncharacteristically pale. Ellie was next to him, wearing her pajamas under a long coat, her eyes red from crying. They were holding hands.

The Lord Chamberlain stepped forward, stiff in his formal attire. "Sir, I'm sorry to tell you, but . . ." The old man's voice faltered for the briefest moment. "The king, your father, is dead."

For the second time that night, Alfie's legs rocked beneath him and he sat down on the thick carpet of the staircase. He felt like he was being pulled into a long tunnel, the Lord Chamberlain's words echoing in his ears from somewhere very far away. The old man bowed his head. The rest of the staff followed suit.

"Your Majesty."

- EIGHT -

The Secret Tunnel

Alfie was underwater. At least, that's what it felt like. Courtiers and officials buzzed around him. Doors opened and slammed. Fragments of muffled conversation reached his ears—*the king has suffered a heart attack . . . But how lucky to die in his own bed . . . The flag must be lowered to half-mast at once . . .* The Lord Chamberlain's pale, craggy face was talking to him in urgent tones about press releases, official periods of mourning, the new king making a formal address to the nation. It took Alfie a moment to realize the old man was talking about him.

I'm king now. The thought sprang into his head and he tried to hide his panic. *But I don't want to be king! I'm not ready! This wasn't supposed to happen so soon!* It was like someone had pressed his life's fast-forward button and skipped to the faraway part he didn't want to know about.

"Are you quite all right, Majesty?" The Lord Chamberlain scowled down at him.

"LC. Do me a favor. Please don't call me that."

The old man winced like he'd been slapped. A footman hurried in, bowed at Alfie, and handed LC a note. He read it and frowned.

"Sir, Prince Richard requests that you attend Princess Eleanor in her chambers. It appears Her Highness is in some distress."

Alfie translated the sentence into plain English—his sister was in her bedroom and was really upset—and rushed off without saying a word.

When he got to Ellie's room he found Richard sitting on the bed, cradling his sister's head on his shoulder as she cried. Alfie hovered nearby, uncertain what to do.

"This is all *her* fault."

Her brothers knew who she meant. Ellie had firmly sided with their dad during the dark days of their parents' divorce. She had refused to talk to their mother, Tamara, for a whole year now. Alfie didn't blame Ellie, but she was too young to know there were two sides to every story.

"That selfish cow destroyed our family and now she's destroyed him!"

Alfie tried to say it was nobody's fault—a freak heart attack—but he couldn't get a word in edgewise as Ellie cried herself out. He tried to hug her, but she shrugged him off.

"Stop pretending like you care. You hated him too." She spat the words at him.

"Come on, Ellie, you don't mean that," said Richard.

She didn't answer, just buried her face in Richard's shirt and sobbed. Alfie decided to leave him to it—his brother was better at handling stuff like this anyway.

Alfie wandered the wide halls of the palace in a daze, past rooms full of officials talking in grave whispers and footmen carrying freshly brewed coffee to keep them working through the night. Everyone he passed gave him a respectful bow and a sympathetic smile. But there was something searching in their looks as well. *So this is our new king? I wonder if he's up to it?*

He found himself alone in the long corridor leading to his father's bedroom. Was Ellie right? Had he hated his own dad? No. But he'd hated what he'd become. What the job had done to him. The job that was now Alfie's. For life. How was he supposed to—

"SHIELD WALL!"

Alfie was suddenly somewhere else, outside in the open air on a rain-swept field, looking out over a sea of helmets, soldiers formed into rows. The men raised their round shields and, in deep voices, cried as one, "Out, out, out!"

"HOLD FAST!"

The command came from Alfie, but it was not his

voice. He was sitting high up on a white horse. He could feel its stone-hard muscles shift beneath him as its hooves slid in the mud. But this was not his body. From across the muddy field, a mass of fair-haired savages in chain mail were charging toward him, painted faces wild with rage, each thick arm holding an ax aloft, a tide of blades sweeping his way. Vikings. This was not Alfie's battle, but he was some-how here and he was scared.

The impact of the Viking attack rocked his men back on their heels. Hacking iron axes split wood and felled the unlucky, but the shield wall held as Alfie's men fought back with their own swords.

"HOLD THE WALL!" Alfie found himself shout-ing. He wanted to turn and run, to get as far as he could from this horrible battle. But instead he galloped into the fight, drawing his sword with a blinding flash—

Alfie snapped awake, the smell of blood and mud sharp in his nostrils. He was back in the palace, gripping the wall for support. What was that? Had he fallen asleep? No, that was more than a dream. It felt real. Alfie glanced back down the long, dark corridor. That feeling he'd had on the playing field at school before the helicopter arrived returned again: eyes in the darkness, searching for him; something powerful he couldn't quite see coming his way.

Thump-thump. The sound was coming from his father's bedroom. Alfie put his ear to the door.

"Hello?"

THUMP-THUMP!

Wary, he eased open the door. A shaft of light fell across his father's large four-poster bed. It didn't look like anyone had slept in it. Would they really have made the bed that quickly?

"Who's there?"

Silence. The room was still. Maybe there was no one there after all. Alfie exhaled. Then he bit down on a scream as something leapt at him out of the darkness. He fell onto his back as heavy feet pressed against his chest. Ragged, rotten meat-breath washed over his face. Shaggy fur brushed against him. A rough tongue licked his cheek.

"Herne?! Down, boy, DOWN!" Alfie shouted and got to his feet, expecting his dad's old dog to snap at him like he had so many times in the past. But, instead, the lanky hound wagged his tail (*thump, thump* against the door) and sat down in front of him, obedient.

Alfie mustered a weary laugh. "What? You *like* me now?"

Still nervous, Alfie reached out and stroked him. The dog rolled over, exposing his belly to be tickled.

"The king is dead. Long live the king, eh?" A voice from the dark behind him. Alfie spun around. How many people could hide in an empty room anyway? He scrambled to turn on the light switch.

The Lord Chamberlain was standing in the corner of the bedroom. "Good evening, Majesty."

"WHERE DID YOU COME FROM?!"

By way of an answer, LC simply stepped to one side. The heavy antique dressing table, which had been against the wall, had moved, revealing a large hole. Beyond it, a spiral stone staircase led down.

The Lord Chamberlain tapped his watch. "Only a few hours till dawn. So if you don't mind, sir, we should get going."

With that, LC disappeared down the steps, leaving Alfie gawking at the secret passage. The old man's head popped back up. "I really *must* insist."

• • •

Alfie pawed the cold stone wall as he followed the Lord Chamberlain deeper and deeper down the spiral staircase. There was no rail to hold on to, and he didn't like the idea of falling into the dark abyss below them. Recessed torches burst into life seemingly of their own accord as they passed by, then somehow extinguished themselves again.

"I don't understand. Is this some sort of security drill?" he asked.

"In a manner of speaking," replied LC.

Water dripped from the stalactites that lined the ceiling, catching Alfie on the back of his neck. "Where are we?"

"Approximately one hundred and fifty feet beneath the streets of London, Your Majesty."

"This is stupid. I'm going back, in case Ellie needs me."

"Not far now!"

At the bottom of the steps the passage opened up into a wide, arched tunnel. Alfie watched, puzzled, as LC reached into an alcove and pulled some unseen lever.

The sound of scraping rock made Alfie jump back. Two giant flagstones slid aside, and a carriage rose out of the floor. Four wooden wheels—the front pair larger than those at the back—faded golden livery, and worn, red-velvet interior: It was just like one of the royal stagecoaches Alfie had seen his father use on state occasions. But there were no horses to pull it and the rickety vehicle had seen much better days. LC opened the door. Alfie looked at him. "Seriously?"

The Lord Chamberlain smiled a tolerant smile. "It's rather a trek otherwise."

Inside the carriage there were two bench seats opposite each other, lit by an old-fashioned gas lamp. LC sat with his back to the empty cab and pulled a padded bar down over himself, like he was settling in for a fairground ride. Alfie was about to ask why this otherwise ancient-looking carriage was fitted with something that wouldn't be out of place on a roller coaster when he noticed that the old man had pulled out a sheaf of official-looking paperwork and was casually flicking through it. Alfie pulled his own bar down.

The carriage rolled sedately forward, to the mouth of a narrower tunnel. The passageway was bare, apart from a steel rail halfway up each wall, running off into the darkness. A *clunk* from somewhere below was loud enough to make Alfie grip his seat. He peered out just in time to see the wheels dislodge themselves and travel up the outside of the carriage, coming to rest horizontally. Each pair sat snug against the rails on the tunnel walls.

Without warning, the carriage surged forward, pinning Alfie back in his seat. Straining to see out of the window, he could just make out the spinning wheels, fringed by crackling, bright blue light, like a miniature electrical storm. The wheels shrieked against the rails as the carriage reached its cruising speed, rocketing down the tunnel. Alfie gaped at the Lord Chamberlain, who was still reading his papers with the quiet determination of a commuter on a rush-hour train. The carriage took a sudden violent left turn, pressing Alfie's body hard into the corner. He let out a high-pitched yelp. A second later it lurched hard to the right, burying Alfie into the other corner.

Alfie was just regaining his breath when the carriage tilted back and shot upward, almost vertically. Some of LC's papers fell over Alfie's face, blinding him for a moment before he found the strength to lift one of his arms against the g-force and pull them away. At last the carriage slowed and they leveled out once more.

"Sorry about the rather sharp turns, sir. Couple of large plague pits down here—best to avoid them." The Lord Chamberlain calmly folded his papers and replaced them in his jacket pocket.

Clunk-clunk. The wheels retracted from the rails and returned to the undercarriage as they rolled serenely to a halt.

LC lifted up his safety bar and opened the carriage door. "After you, sir."

Alfie stumbled out on jelly legs and looked around. They were inside a small, dimly lit chamber. Somewhere far above them a clock struck the hour. A scratching sound drew Alfie's attention to a nearby raven, which was pecking at a jumbo-sized pretzel. Sensing it was being watched, the bird emitted an indignant *gronk!* and carried its supper away to a more private corner.

"Is this . . . ?"

"The Tower. Yes, sir."

"Of London?"

The Lord Chamberlain allowed himself a wry smile. "Indeed."

LC crossed to a huge vaulted oak door at the far end. Alfie rubbed his arms against the cold and scurried after him.

"I've been to the Tower before and I don't remember anything about secret tunnels or magic carriages."

"This is . . . the *other* Tower."

The Lord Chamberlain removed a heavy, silver-tipped staff from a mount on the wall, raised it above his head, and pounded on the great door three times.

- NINE -

The Other Tower

Alfie couldn't believe what he was seeing. He was standing with LC at one end of a vast underground hall. The windowless stone walls were draped with enormous tapestries depicting some of the most famous events in British history. Except that these were *not* the versions he had been taught at school: He did not recall the Spanish Armada of 1588 being sunk by a gigantic squid; he had thought the Great Fire of London in 1666 was started by a careless baker, not a fearsome red dragon; and if there had been a rampaging army of ogres at the Battle of Waterloo in 1815, he was pretty sure he'd have remembered hearing about it. But that wasn't all. In each woven image, right in the thick of the action, was a sword-wielding knight in sleek white armor flying on a phantom horse.

"Hey, isn't that the fake superhero guy from the papers? You know—the Defender."

"Ah, you've heard of him, good." LC smiled. "That will save some time."

The low hum of industrious work echoed around the great chamber. The main floor was covered with an enormous mosaic of a Tudor rose painted a brilliant red. Positioned in each petal was a cluster of heavy oak desks, each manned by a beefeater. There were maybe twenty of them in all, mainly gray-haired and stocky. Most were men with bushy beards, although Alfie noticed a couple of women too, bustling around in their traditional scarlet-and-black tunics. There was not a computer in sight. A network of transparent pneumatic tubes ran above the desks, delivering capsules that whizzed to and fro. Once in the hands of a beef-eater, the capsules were cracked open and their contents unloaded by the recipient, before being sucked back into the pipes again. On every desk were old-fashioned phones with large enamel receivers in bright red, white, and blue, which rang intermittently.

"What is this place?" asked Alfie.

"We call it the Keep," replied LC.

The Lord Chamberlain struck his staff on the floor. The beefeaters turned to them and stood at attention, as one.

"GOD SAVE THE KING!"

The force of their cry startled Alfie. He felt like they were waiting for him to say something.

"Um . . . thanks?"

LC gave a slight nod of his head and the beef-eaters returned to their work. Alfie scurried down the wide stone steps and followed LC through the hall. At its center sat a grand table-map of Britain, the size of four pool tables pushed together. It was carved from wood and dotted with ornate icons representing a host of important national sites—Wembley Stadium, Sizewell B nuclear power station, the Forth Bridge—as well as the locations of ancient castles and battlefields—Corfe, Bosworth, Dover. Alfie paused to watch a beefeater wearing bulky black headphones push a little lead model of a lizard man to the place on the map marking Stonehenge.

"This is the Map Room, Majesty," said LC. "The operations table helps us keep an eye on what's going on in the kingdom." He spoke as if it was the most natural thing in the world to be monitoring—what?—*monsters*?!

Alfie realized what this place reminded him of: the Cabinet War Rooms—the bunker in Whitehall, now a museum, where they had re-created the headquarters from which Churchill had conducted Britain's Second World War operations. Except that *there* the figures sitting at desks gazing at maps and manila folders were dummies. *Here* they were living, breathing men and women, most of them with pretty impressive beards.

"What are the beefeaters doing here in the middle of the night, LC?"

"They prefer 'yeoman warders,' sir. And they are Your Majesty's bodyguard. They are never off duty."

"I thought Brian was my bodyguard? Speaking of which, does he even know we're—"

"'Fraid so, boss."

It was Brian, pushing an ancient-looking stone casket on an upright trolley. Its surface was covered with a carving of the Defender. He stopped and pulled a startled Alfie into a hug. "Sorry about your dad. He was a good bloke."

LC frowned. "A little decorum when around His Majesty, if you please."

Brian pushed the trolley away. "It's only a man hug. Don't get your tights in a twist."

"They're called breeches. You know they are, because I've corrected you on that point several times before." LC composed himself and ushered Alfie on through the hall. "Brian may be rather unconventional, but his skills as the king's armorer make up for it. Just about."

"I have an armorer?" Alfie asked, perplexed.

"One thing at a time, Majesty."

The old man guided him through a thick velvet curtain and into a private alcove, lit by candles.

Alfie saw that he was standing on a giant engraving of his family's coat of arms—a white shield adorned with a blue cross, held on one side by a black swan and on the other by a red boar. Beneath it was the House of Arundel's motto: *Non ducor, duco. I am not led, I lead.*

But the last thing Alfie felt like right now was a leader. "LC, tell me what's going on. What is all this? What am I doing here?"

The Lord Chamberlain fixed him with an intense stare. He seemed nervous, which wasn't something Alfie was used to seeing. "Sir, your father did not die of a heart attack. He was killed. In battle."

Alfie laughed. "Battle? What are you talking about? What battle?"

With great ceremony, the Lord Chamberlain produced an ornate key and unlocked an ancient carved cupboard. Alfie, curious, strained to see, but the old man stepped aside anyway to reveal a dusty television and an ancient-looking video recorder. He took a videotape from his jacket, inserted it into the machine with a loud clunk, and turned on the TV. Static fuzzed on the screen. Then LC punched a couple of buttons. Nothing happened.

"Every time," tutted LC.

A beefeater leaned through a curtain. "You need to stick it on channel six."

Alfie looked from side to side, bewildered, as another beefeater popped in. "Make sure the plug hasn't come loose at the back."

LC had put on a pair of reading glasses and was flicking through a moth-eaten instruction manual.

Brian barged in and smacked the VCR on the top. Sure enough, the screen cleared. "If in doubt, give it a whack."

Before Alfie knew it, everyone else had melted away and he was alone in the alcove. He felt his way around the dark curtains, but could not find a gap. It was as if the drapes had become a wall. There was no way through, no way under.

"Alfred."

His father's voice. Alfie spun around, almost losing his footing. There he was on the TV screen, King Henry, sitting by the fireplace in one of the palace drawing rooms. He was addressing the camera, like he was giving one of his boring Christmas broadcasts.

"If you are watching this, then it means I am gone and you have taken my place as king. If this has happened while you are still young, then I am truly sorry. The burdens you now carry are not something a young man should have to bear."

Even from beyond the grave he was struggling to drop the formal tone, thought Alfie.

"Unlike most people, you have always known your destiny. And I realize that has not been easy. But there are some things you do not know—things that now you must learn. For a thousand years the head of our family has been the custodian of certain powers, passed down through our bloodline. Not merely symbolic, empty titles as you might think. These are real, unique abilities that have been used at times of crisis to protect our nation and its people. This great kingdom has more enemies than you can possibly imagine . . ."

Alfie thought about the giant tapestries hanging in the hall with all the fantastical monsters. Could they be real?

His father continued. "At the moment I died, you became king. But you also became something else: *Defender of the Realm*. That has been your true destiny since the day you were born, and I believe it is yours for a reason. There are those who will help you become accustomed to your new role: faithful and wise allies. Listen to them. But in the end, know that the power growing inside you is a lonely gift. Only you can decide how to use it. Duty is not something you do because you are told to; it is something you do because you believe it to be right. I have done my duty to the best of my ability since the night I stood where you stand now, but there are things I wish I had done differently—so much I could have done better. I love you, Alfred. Good luck, my son."

The image of his father disappeared and the screen returned to a storm of static. Alfie's feet felt as if they had become one with the floor, as if he were turning into just another statue that would remain rooted there forever.

Behind him the curtain parted once more, and the Lord Chamberlain stepped back into the alcove. He laid a hand on Alfie's shoulder. Alfie flinched as if stung. There were tears in his eyes. "Why are you doing this to me?" he whispered.

He pushed past the Lord Chamberlain and bolted back into the hall. He didn't know where he was going, but he needed space to think. He needed to get away from all this madness. LC strode after him, surprisingly quick on his long legs, catching up with Alfie amid the maze of beefeaters' desks. "Your Majesty, please wait—"

But Alfie didn't want to hear any more. "My father was no hero. He couldn't even kick a ball in a straight line! I never even saw him ride a bike! You expect me to believe he could fly through the sky at will?"

"Of course not, sir. His *horse* flew; he merely rode it."

Alfie let out a hollow laugh and looked around the chamber at the beefeaters. They were doing their best to carry on with their work, but he could tell they were all listening. He marched back to the door and pulled at the iron handle, to no avail.

"Could somebody tell me what special code I need to get out of this place?" Alfie shouted and waved his hand angrily at the locked door.

Suddenly he felt a rush of blood to his head, heard his pulse loud in his ears, and the door flew open with a bang that echoed around the hall. Shocked, he gazed at his palm and saw the veins in his hand glow blue beneath his skin for a moment.

The Lord Chamberlain watched, disappointed, as Alfie ran out into the tunnel without looking back. Brian strolled over to join him. "Go easy on the boy; he's just lost his dad."

The Lord Chamberlain gazed back at the ops table and the figurine of the Black Lizard next to Stonehenge. "We don't have time. He needs to be ready."

TEN

Intruders

Hayley hurried out from the shadow of the tower block, heading for Barron's corner shop. She didn't like leaving her gran alone in the apartment too long when she was having one of her bad days. And yet she couldn't help pausing to glance up at the sky, half hoping to catch sight of a white knight zooming past on a ghostly horse. The world felt very different now that she knew there was something beyond school—beyond chores and potatoes for dinner. She was desperate to cling on to that feeling, for a while longer at least.

As Hayley scooted past, lost in her thoughts, cold eyes watched her from the car still parked across the street.

"Finally," muttered Turpin, reaching into the glove box to remove a small pistol. "I thought she'd never go out."

Fulcher woke up and wiped a line of drool from her chin. She eyed her partner's gun with disdain. "Scared of old women?" she chuckled.

"You do what you want. I'm not taking any

chances," snapped Turpin as he pocketed the pistol and opened the car door.

In the corner shop, Hayley tossed a box of tea bags onto the counter. Behind the till, Dean Barron was busy looking at his hair in the mirror and tapping his foot (out of time) to hip-hop blaring from his phone's tiny speaker. He had a very high forehead and his wispy hair was already receding. Dean's dad, who owned the shop, was completely bald, and Dean was obviously worried he was destined to go the same way. He was as obsessed with his looks as he was with his customized Peugeot hatchback, which was parked outside as usual. It was a hideous lime green with bucket seats and an oversized spoiler. Hayley thought it looked like a Quality Street chocolate on wheels. And the horrible thing was loud too; she could hear its thundering engine all the way from the fourteenth floor when Dean and his mates drove it around the estate at night.

Coins clattered onto the counter as Hayley poured pennies out of a small plastic bag. She had a large change jar at home, which she'd filled up just by keeping her eyes locked on the ground when she was walking to and from school. It never ceased to amaze her that people were practically throwing money away. She had counted out exactly the amount she needed for the tea bags and not a penny more—that way she wouldn't be tempted to buy anything they didn't really need.

"What's this?" exclaimed Dean, throwing up his hands.

Hayley smiled. "Money. It's all there. I counted. Hope you can too."

Dean grimaced back at her. "Seen any big lizard monsters today, Hayley?"

Dean and his so-called gang (they called themselves the "Watford Massive") must have been having a good laugh about what Hayley's gran had said to the neighbors. Hayley stopped herself from blurting out some of the rude words that flashed through her mind (she didn't want to get banned from the shop—the nearest supermarket was three miles away). Instead, while Dean made a point of counting every single penny, Hayley decided to check the rack of newspapers. Maybe there would be a story about the Defender's battle at the Tower by now—that would shut up stupid Dean Ba—

Her thought was interrupted as she caught sight of the front pages. They were strangely solemn and uniform—even the tabloids had black banners instead of their usual garish red. Every one bore a picture of the king. The headlines were plain and bold: KING DEAD; BRITAIN MOURNS; REST IN PEACE, YOUR MAJESTY. The only paper not leading with the story had gone instead with some bizarre report about Stonehenge collapsing in a freak earthquake.

Hayley grabbed the nearest paper and skimmed the first few lines—*King Henry suffered a heart attack late last night . . . Princes Alfred and Richard and Princess Eleanor rushed back to the palace . . . Prince Alfred is now King Alfred II . . . Coronation to take place in a few weeks' time . . .*

"This ain't a library," Dean sneered.

But all Hayley cared about was getting back to the apartment as quickly as she could. If Gran had turned on the radio she might have heard the news already, and Hayley couldn't bear the idea of not being there to comfort her if she was upset.

"Like you'd know what the inside of a library looks like," she said as she snatched the tea bags and bolted from the shop, leaving Dean red-faced.

"Oi, I'm not finished counting yet . . . It better all be here!"

Hayley was back home in less than a minute. As she let herself in, she could hear a man's voice coming from the living room—Gran must be watching TV, which meant she was too late. But as she hurried into the room she realized it wasn't the news she could hear. It was a strange little man perched on the edge of the sofa.

"It's all quite routine of course, madam," said Turpin, smiling.

Fulcher filled the other two-thirds of the sofa next to him. Hayley instinctively took a step back when she saw her. She felt like she had just come face to face with a wild animal and any sudden movement might spark a vicious attack.

"Here she is. Here's my Hayley," said Gran, beckoning her over. "I've been telling these nice detectives all about what a good girl you are, looking after your silly old grandmother."

As Hayley sat next to her gran, she eased her hands into her pockets, doing her best to conceal any sign of the alarm bells that were shrieking inside her head. Whoever this odd pair was, Hayley knew one thing for sure: They weren't police.

"I was just telling your grandmother here how sorry we are that we didn't come sooner," continued Turpin, grinning at her with his unnaturally white teeth, "but there was a great deal of tidying up to do at the Tower after the, um, incident."

"The Tower?" asked Hayley.

"I told them we were right there, dear," her gran said. "Saw the whole thing, clear as a bell."

Fulcher had not averted her heavy gaze from Hayley since the moment she'd walked in. Hayley got the distinct impression that the huge woman would happily crush her neck with one of her gargantuan hands if she made the wrong move.

"Our concern, Miss Hicks," Turpin went on, "is that you may have been exposed to materials—hazardous biological materials—which could do you serious harm if you were to have, say, accidentally brought them home with you . . ." His little black eyes scanned the room before returning to Hayley.

"We wouldn't want to get ill, would we, Hales?" said Gran.

"Don't worry, Gran. I'm sure we didn't *accidentally* bring anything back with us. Thank you for checking on us, though, detectives."

Turpin's smile faded. He gave an almost imperceptible nod of the head to Fulcher, who rose from her seat like a whale breaching the surface of a calm sea and began to clomp around the room, nosing into shelves and sweeping her hands behind the furniture.

"You can't do that!" shouted Hayley.

"Please, Miss Hicks, this is for your own safety."

A framed photo crashed to the floor as Fulcher's thick arms rooted around the back of the sideboard.

"What's happening, Hayley?" Her gran was becoming upset.

"All right! I'll give you what you want. Just don't break anything else."

Hayley led Fulcher out of the room while Turpin stayed sitting with her confused gran.

"Unseasonably cold for the time of year . . ." Hayley heard Turpin making small talk once more as she walked down the hall, shadowed by the hulking agent.

In her bedroom, Hayley opened the wardrobe and stood to one side. "It's in there."

"Get it, then," growled Fulcher.

But Hayley shook her head. "You said it was dangerous—I don't want to touch it."

The giant woman grumbled and pushed past Hayley, leaning down and reaching an arm into the wardrobe. "Where is it? You better not be mucking about."

"In a bag, right at the back."

Fulcher groaned as she got down on all fours and poked her head between the clothes, feeling around with her hands in the darkness.

Behind her, Hayley dashed forward, planting one foot on a chair and launching herself at the wardrobe. She grabbed on to the top and used her weight to pull the whole thing over onto the kneeling woman.

A roar erupted from beneath the downed wardrobe, but Hayley was already sprinting back into the living room. Turpin had just enough time to get to his feet after hearing the crash, but Hayley was too quick for him—she rammed her gran's walking stick into his chest and sent him toppling back over the sofa.

Hayley grabbed her gran and eased her as fast as she dared onto her feet and into the hall.

"Where are we going, Hales? We've got guests!"

"Bit of fresh air, Gran?!"

They reached the door, but suddenly Gran turned back. "I'll need my coat."

"NO, GRAN!"

Hayley lost her grip as Gran disappeared into the kitchen. A shower of broken wood exploded from Hayley's bedroom and Fulcher was there, charging at her like an angry rhino. The brute grabbed Hayley in a bear hug and lifted her off the ground. Hayley screamed and kicked out as hard as she could, turning over a side table and smashing a mirror, but there was no escape.

"You little moron!" yelled Fulcher, veins bulging in her tree-trunk neck.

Turpin slid out of the living room, rubbing his chest. "No need for that, Fulcher." He pointed his pistol at Hayley.

Fulcher put Hayley down as Gran returned to the hall, buttoning up her coat. "Ready! Oh, are you two coming as well?"

Sirens sounded from outside. Turpin frowned and hurried to the window. Two police cars had pulled up in front of the flats below, blue lights flashing. Policemen were rushing into the building. He turned back to Hayley, his face darkening. "What did you do?"

Hayley smiled. "What's wrong? I thought you said you were police too?"

Turpin reached into Hayley's pocket and pulled out a cell phone. It was connected; the number on the screen: 9-9-9. He screamed and turned to smash the phone against the wall, but Hayley snatched it back, holding it out of his reach.

Fulcher tried to grab Hayley again, but Turpin held her back. He fixed Hayley with a cold stare. "We'll be seeing you again," he hissed. "Soon."

And with that, the pair of them left.

Hayley just had time to steer her gran away from the wreckage of the hallway and back into the living room before the police arrived. The *real* police.

• • •

Hours later, after Gran had been checked out at the hospital—and once Hayley had talked to a steady stream of doctors and nurses and social workers, tidied up the flat, and settled Gran down for a nap—she finally returned to her room. Unscrewing the back of an old hollow desktop computer she'd salvaged, she fished out the lizard's scale and smiled to herself. She had decided the night before that it needed a better hiding place than inside her backpack. *Good thing too*, she thought. She tossed the scale into her backpack and, checking that there was no sign of the two intruders from earlier—whoever the hell they really were—she made her way outside to the tower block roof.

There, amid the rusting water tanks and pipes, Hayley found a forgotten rooftop garden and an old plant bed full of foul-smelling soil mixed with pigeon droppings. She dug a hole as deep as she could, then pulled out the black scale from her backpack. The dark lines on its surface seemed to pulse in the moonlight. Why hadn't she just handed it over to them? It wasn't really hers, after all. Why risk getting herself—or worse, her gran—hurt over something she couldn't even begin to understand? And yet . . . she couldn't just forget what she had seen that night at the Tower. She'd had a glimpse of something from another world—something magical. She had to know more. Somehow she knew that if she gave up the scale, her only solid link to that strange world, then she would never get any answers.

Hayley pushed the black scale deep into the rank earth and covered it over.

- ELEVEN -

Made in the United Kingdom

Escape.

It was the only word in Alfie's overcrowded head that made any sense right now. He had to get out: out of this corridor, out of the palace, and just to be on the safe side, probably out of the country as well.

Herne trotted behind him as he ran, easily keeping up. "Herne, no!" Alfie hissed. "Go away. Bed. Away!" But the dog just cocked his head and stared. He wasn't going anywhere. "OK, fine. Just don't bite anyone."

It was early and Alfie kept to the maze of quieter back stairs, ducking out of the way every time he heard a footman or maid approaching. Finally he made it to a side entrance that opened out onto the palace's inner courtyard and the Ambassadors' Entrance. Official cars were starting to arrive, dropping off solemn-looking men and women who were no doubt there to plan his father's funeral.

Alfie shuddered, but forced himself to focus and wait until the right moment to make a break for it.

A convoy of cars pulled up to the entrance and another large delegation of suits swept up the steps. With the guards' backs briefly turned, Alfie eased open the door and crept out. Keeping low, and with Herne at his heels, he threaded his way through the parked cars and made it to one of the waiting black Daimlers, its engine still idling. Alfie threw himself in and sat low with Herne on the backseat.

"Take me to a train station. I don't care which."

It was true. Alfie didn't have a plan other than to find some space to think, away from the palace.

The chauffeur didn't turn around and the car didn't move.

"Um, excuse me. I'm the king. The new one? I'm pretty sure what I say goes. So, um . . . let's go."

"No problem," came the gruff voice from the front seat, "I'll just need to arrange some motorcycle outriders. And a follow car, full of protection officers. That's after we've conducted a risk assessment of the route, of course—swept for devices, closed the garbage cans, checked the sewers, blah-di-blah. And we'll need to put air support on standby. Oh, and clear it with the Home Office. Shouldn't take more than five or six hours." The "chauffeur" turned around, grinning. It was Brian. "Maybe we should go inside and talk?"

Alfie leapt out of the car and ran, plowing through the huddle of people gathered on the steps of the Ambassadors' Entrance. "Coming through!" he shouted as everyone bowed, bewildered, making space for him to bustle past. "Sorry, excuse me!"

"Majesty, wait!" A worried-looking LC rushed down the grand staircase toward him, trying to head him off, but Alfie threw open a door and ran along a service passage. He was making the escape route up as he went along, but he knew this way led to the kitchens, a busy back entrance at the far end, and an exit onto Constitution Hill. Maybe he could snag a cab, or a bus—anything to get away. He sprinted through the kitchens, dodging between surprised chefs making breakfast and shocked servants carrying trays of tea. Herne lolloped behind, enjoying the exercise.

But when Alfie reached the kitchen exit, the door was locked and Brian was perched at a counter next to it, tucking into a bacon sandwich.

"You really should have some grub, you know. Bacon makes everything seem better." Brian offered him a bite.

"Just leave me alone!" Alfie yelled, then he backed away and just ran, down corridors, up staircases, and through hallways at random: a headlong charge, trying to find any other way out. But if Harrow was a prison, then Buckingham Palace was a maximum-security fortress. On an island. Surrounded by sharks. He'd never get out, he'd never escape, he'd never—

Hands grasped his shoulders, bringing him to a sudden halt. "Alfie?"

It was Richard, his face full of concern at his brother's wild appearance. Alfie felt relief wash over him.

"Richie, you're not going to believe what's happened. It's just incredible. Dad, he was the king, right? But he wasn't *just* the king. You know?"

Richard studied his brother's face, puzzled. "Are you all right?"

"OK, let me start again . . ." Alfie thought about it. How could he even begin to tell his brother what he'd seen at the Keep? "I've got to show you something." He grabbed Richard's arm and dragged him back down the hallway to their father's bedroom.

"This is going to blow your mind right out of its skull. I mean, seriously, BOOM! Get this—there's a tunnel under here!"

With a grunt, Alfie moved the dressing table to reveal . . . carpet. He looked at Richard, panicked. "I swear to you, it was right here!" Alfie fell to his knees and smacked his fists against the floor in frustration.

"Alfie?" Richard was trying his best to sound calm.

"There's this supersonic carriage! And an army of beefeaters that live underground!" Alfie was pulling at the carpet. "And an armorer."

"Stop. Please."

"And Dad was there—I mean, he wasn't really; it was a tape of him on this old video player that didn't really work properly—but, anyway, he was telling me all this mad stuff—"

"ALFIE!"

It wasn't Richard's shouting that stopped Alfie from raving: It was the look on his face. *He thinks I've totally lost it.*

Richard strode over to Alfie and pulled him to his feet. "You can't just freak out like this. Get it together. People are relying on you. *I'm* relying on you."

"But you don't understand," Alfie said, suddenly miserable and exhausted. "Something's happened. Something big."

"Well, yeah." Richard pulled Alfie in for a hug. "You're the king now."

• • •

The next few days were a blur. Because Alfie was still underage it meant that, as well as being Lord Chamberlain, the ancient fun-free zone was also now officially the "Lord Protector." It was his job to guide and mentor the new young king through his duties until he turned eighteen. As far as Alfie could tell, what this meant was that the old guy was stuck to him like glue 24/7. There were papers to sign, people's hands to shake, weird rules to learn, and every minute of the day there was some new instruction he needed to follow or some royal duty he needed to perform. And whenever he and LC were alone together, the old man was very keen to talk to Alfie about what had happened in the Keep.

"Sir, we really must talk about all the *other* business."

But Alfie would find a way to avoid the conversation by calling a servant for some urgent tea, inviting someone else in, or, on more than one occasion, just running out of the room. "Another time, LC!"

Everyone in the palace was busy marshaling preparations for his father's state funeral. There would be thousands of guests from every nation on earth arriving in London: VIPs, prime ministers, presidents, kings and queens—they would all be there. In the streets outside the palace, soldiers, cavalry, and pipe bands practiced their parts in the procession day and night. TV cameras were placed to cover every angle of the funeral procession's route to Westminster Abbey. The Lord Chamberlain told Alfie that, although it was his father's funeral, he mustn't forget that everyone would be looking at him, watching his every movement, waiting to see if he would stumble. *Thanks*, thought Alfie, *like I wasn't freaking out enough already.*

All week the press had given Alfie a hard time— "King Alfred the Not So Great" they called him (Alfie could just imagine how smug Mortimer would be when he read that one). The boy king would be such a disaster that what remained of the monarchy would come crumbling down within a year, the pundits predicted. The funny thing was, Alfie kind of agreed with them—he even hoped they were right. At least it would get him off the hook.

Alfie sat in the study watching the clock tick around to twelve a.m. It felt strange to be sitting at his dad's old desk. He'd seen his father hunched over it so many times, and here he was, doing the same. Across the dark expanse of St. James's Park, Big Ben solemnly chimed the hour. Alfie took a shaky breath. Today was one of those days you couldn't get out of. There was no sick note and no running away this time. Today he was burying his dad. Alfie was just going through the million different ways he could screw up in front of the entire world when the phone on the desk rang. He knew who it was before he'd even picked it up. There was only one person who would call him in the middle of the night.

"Hello, Mother."

"Did I wake you up, Alf? What time is it there?"

Tamara—or Queen Tamara, as she had been known before the divorce—always forgot about the seven-hour time difference between Wyoming and London. Alfie's mum was American born and bred. She had met King Henry twenty-five years ago, back when his dad was just a prince and Tamara was just plain old "Tammy" Rhodes, working on a ranch he happened to be visiting. They'd fallen in love and it was the ultimate fairy tale. FROM COWPOKE TO PRINCESS! TAMMY LASSOS HER PRINCE! It was more complicated than that, of course—she was a qualified veterinary nurse, for a start, who specialized in horses—but it was hands down the planet's favorite love story for years. Until the messy divorce, that is.

"Don't worry about it, Mum."

"I'm sorry I haven't called for a while. It's just been . . . Oh, I'm really sorry. About everything."

The connection was so terrible, she might as well have been calling from Mars. After the divorce, Alfie's mum had gone back home and into hiding to avoid the press. She'd bought a cabin in the middle of nowhere—even Alfie didn't quite know where it was, it was so far off the map. She'd taken to writing old-fashioned, snail-mail letters, detailing the abundant wildlife, telling him about hearing wolves howling in winter and not seeing people for days. It sounded pretty good to Alfie right now.

"Listen, Mum, I need to ask you something. When you and Dad were together, did he ever tell you anything about what he was really up to?"

"How do you mean?"

"Did he tell you anything about the job?" Alfie was floundering but pushed on. "Special duties? That kind of thing. Weird stuff, you know?"

"Sweetie, it's the monarchy. It was all pretty weird to me. That's kind of why we split up."

It was true; she'd never really fit into the royal family, with all its stuffy rules and ancient etiquette. Alfie's mum had hit the palace like a force of nature, all high spirits and fun, but within a few years it had broken her, and she'd limped home and out of sight like one of the injured animals she used to tend.

"Oh, Alf, I wish I could be there for you today, really I do. But you know I'd just be a distraction. Those London papers hate me, and I don't want to make it harder on you than it already is. Come and see me sometime?"

Alfie sighed inwardly. They both knew that wasn't going to happen anytime soon, but he played along anyway. "OK, Mum, I will."

"And don't let that old fart push you around either." One thing they had always agreed on was how much they couldn't stand the Lord Chamberlain.

"I should get some sleep," said Alfie. "Big day."

Alfie thought he heard a sigh on the other end of the line, but his mother didn't argue. "Thinking of you. Always."

Alfie hung up and gazed forlornly at the mountain of leather-bound tomes in front of him. LC had given him a stack of boring books to read as homework for his new job. He picked one up at random—Walter Bagehot's *The English Constitution*—opened the first page, then swiftly closed it again and tossed it back on the pile. It missed and sent his father's large fountain pen skidding across the desk and onto the floor.

Alfie knelt down. The pen had rolled under the sofa, and he could just see that it was spilling ink out of its nib onto the carpet. He pressed himself against the sofa's worn edge, the smell of old leather and dust filling his nostrils, and reached out his arm. The pen had rolled too far. He tried to push the sofa back, but it was too heavy to budge. *Great.*

He lay as flat as he could on the carpet and stretched his arm underneath the sofa once more. His fingertip nudged the end of the pen, but only pushed it farther away.

Who still uses a fountain pen anyway? Typical Dad . . .

The muscles in his neck ached as he reached for it one last time, determined not to be defeated.

Out of touch, out of reach, just like this stupid . . . bloody . . . PEN!

In a flash, the pen leapt off the carpet and speared through the bottom of the sofa. Alfie sat up, startled, as the pen burst out of the seat in a shower of cushion filling, hovered in the air for a moment, and then shot straight at him, coming to rest with a *smack* in the palm of his shaking hand.

"WHOA!"

Alfie dropped the pen and jumped back. His hand tingled, like it was charged with electricity. His raised veins glowed blue for an instant, just like when the doors had blown open without him touching them in the Keep. Alfie picked the pen up again. It was silver, heavy but elegant, and five words were engraved on the side in tiny scrolled writing: MADE IN THE UNITED KINGDOM.

"Alfie?"

Alfie jumped. It was Ellie. She was standing at the study door, staring at her brother.

"I couldn't sleep. Are you all right?"

"I'm . . . fine. I'm good. Don't worry."

Ellie smiled, relieved, then noticed the ugly, ink-stained rip in the sofa and the pen in her brother's hand. She stiffened and glared at him. "What are you doing? Why did you do that, Alfie?"

Alfie's head was spinning. "I didn't! At least, I don't think I did. I've been feeling weird recently. Do you think you can be really ill and not know it?"

Feeling faint, Alfie reached out for his sister but she stepped back, angry and confused. "That's really big of you, smashing up Dad's stuff when he's not here to stop you."

"I'm sorry. Can we talk about this tomorrow? I'm just really tired."

"Really crazy, you mean." Ellie stomped out.

Alfie watched her walk away until the gloom of the long corridor swallowed her up. All his little sister had wanted was a hug, for someone to tell her everything was going to be all right. But now she clearly thought he was going mad.

Scary thing is, thought Alfie, *she might be right.*

TWELVE

Blue Blood

The guns boomed their salute across London as Alfie watched the soldiers lift his father's coffin from the carriage and bear it into Westminster Abbey. From the stormy skies above to the plumes on the heads of the horses, London was swathed in black, like the world had been drained of color. Even King Henry's Royal Standard, with its rich blues and yellows, had been lowered for the last time as the procession left the palace, leaving nothing but the bare flagpole, rattling in the wind.

Alfie's brother and sister were standing on either side of him, Richard in his naval cadet uniform, Ellie in an elegant black coat. The girl had a faraway look in her eyes, like she wasn't really taking any of it in. They'd walked behind the cortege at a steady pace, in time with the muffled drums of the massed bands, playing their somber marches.

The crowds were vast and silent, and even though he knew everyone was watching him, Alfie had the now familiar feeling of something else out there, something powerful, magical, and not of this world.

And the more he thought about it, the more the thing seemed to stir and seek him out.

"Alfie?" whispered Richard. "They're ready."

Alfie looked around. The coffin was disappearing into the Abbey. He began to climb the steps, past the guard of honor with their bowed heads—

"SEND THEM ALL TO VALHALLA!"

Alfie was suddenly back on the muddy battlefield, charging on horseback into the mass of Vikings, sweeping aside several of the roaring savages with each swing of his glowing sword. He was carving his way through the melee with ease, his men cheering and yelling as they followed behind. He knew he should feel terrified by the slaughter all around him, but instead he felt unstoppable.

Howls, long and deep, echoed all around. A pack of monstrous black dogs, their coats shaggy and matted with filth, crested the brow of the hill and thundered past their Viking masters, bearing down on Alfie's men.

"SHIELD WALL, HOLD!"

The stampede hit them like a wave, flattening men onto their backs, breaking through shields with tearing teeth, pulling screaming soldiers to pieces. Alfie's horse reared up and tumbled under the assault of the dogs, until he found himself lying in the mud, face to face with one of the hellish hounds, its muzzle thick with spittle and blood, and where its eyes should be, red-hot burning flames—

"ALFIE?!"

Richard and Ellie were standing over him, concerned. Alfie looked around in a daze. He was out of the waking dream and back on the Abbey steps. Well, *sprawled* on the steps where he'd fallen. He was dimly aware of the distant clatter of camera shutters and he knew at once what the headlines would be. But more than anything at that moment, Alfie was aware of how much his hand was throbbing. He must have held it out to break his fall. He looked at it and gasped.

He was bleeding *blue* blood. Dark, royal blue, oozing out of the cut. Alfie lifted his shaking hand so his brother and sister could see.

"Yeah, you fell over." Richard helped him up, keeping his voice low.

"But don't you see?" Alfie pleaded.

Ellie gave him a handkerchief. "What's the big deal?" she hissed. "It's just a scratch."

Alfie looked back at his hand. It *was* just a scratch, and the small amount of blood there had turned back to plain old red.

Richard grabbed Alfie's arm. "Come on, let's get you inside."

• • •

After the ceremony they were driven across a rainy London to the Frogmore estate, the royal burial ground near Windsor Castle, for a further private service. Weeping willows hung low over tranquil ponds, and everywhere around them were the stones marking the graves of Alfie's ancestors. *There could be worse places to spend eternity*, he thought as the mourners gathered to say a final farewell to his father.

Later, as they walked back to the cars, Richard and Ellie were still laughing about one of the priests who had nearly tripped over a headstone during the blessing. It was as if they had permission to relax, now that the grim official business of the day was over. Alfie could only watch them and wish that he were able to feel the same way. He didn't want them to leave, but he'd agreed that it was best for them both to head back to school right away. Richard had a big rugby match the next day and Ellie was going to watch the Oxford and Cambridge Boat Race—she was already planning to go to one of the two universities when she was old enough, so that she could get on the rowing team and try to beat the men's record time. *Knowing Ellie, she'd probably do it too*, thought Alfie.

"How's the hand, Majesty?" Richard asked with a smile.

"Just a scratch," replied Alfie. "Sorry about before at the Abbey. I don't know what happened."

"You freaked out again, that's what happened,"

chipped in Ellie helpfully, as she got into the waiting car. "Just try not to make it so easy for the press, Alf; they've already got it in for you."

Richard put an arm around his brother as they waved good-bye to her. "You must have known this day was going to come, sooner or later," he said.

"Later would have been preferable," said Alfie. "Much, much later—like when I was a hundred years old. Anyway, I can't believe just because I came out ten seconds before you did that I'm the one who gets this dumb job. Who makes up these rules?"

"Well, whoever it was, I'm pleased they did. The family firm is all yours, bro." Richard hopped into the next car and rolled down the window. "Give me a call if I can do anything, yeah? Hang in there, Alfie. I'll see you soon."

Alfie mustered a smile and gave him a wave as the car pulled away. He turned to look for his own car, but there was no sign of it. Brian was hovering at the gates at the far end of the drive, but everyone else seemed to have gone. Alfie was just wondering how the king could be the last person to be picked up when the Lord Chamberlain appeared at his shoulder with an umbrella.

"Apologies, Majesty—a slight delay with your carriage."

Alfie realized he'd been set up. LC had been trying to get him alone for days and he'd finally done it, just when Alfie's guard was down. "You sneaky old . . . Fine, I'll walk."

Ignoring the rain, which was getting heavier again, Alfie began to march off down the path.

"Don't you want to know what's happening to you, sir?" LC called after him.

Alfie stopped. He could feel himself giving in. He didn't know if he could cope with any more insane revelations about his family's little secret, but he had so many questions . . .

They found some shelter under the arches of Queen Victoria's mausoleum. The masonry was cracking and the entrance was clogged with leaves— clearly it didn't receive many visitors these days.

"We call it the Succession, sir. The magical bequeathing of power—real power—from one monarch to the next. The moment your father passed away, the powers he possessed left his body and began to search for a new home, for a successor. For you. It has been that way for centuries."

Alfie shivered, and not just from the cold. LC was describing exactly what he'd felt ever since his dad had died: like something overwhelming was trying to find him and possess him.

"I've been having these strange dreams—except they happen when I'm awake."

"Ancestral memories, carried through the Defender's bloodline. What have you seen in these visions?"

"I don't know. I'm on a horse. There's a battle going on—which I am really enjoying, for some reason. We're fighting these scary blond guys in helmets . . . I think they might be Vikings. Oh, and there's a bunch of nasty-looking giant dogs running around chewing people's heads off. Sweet dreams, huh?"

The Lord Chamberlain didn't seem the least bit surprised. "Ah, the Battle of Edington, 878 AD. Sounds to me like you're seeing through the eyes of your esteemed namesake, Alfred the Great, the original Defender."

"This all started with him?"

"Yes. When Alfred became king, England was already all but lost. The Vikings had invaded with their armies of savages and their devil dogs and driven Alfred and the remnants of his army into hiding."

"I don't remember Professor Lock teaching us about any Viking devil dogs."

"Of course not, sir. This is the *real* history," LC said. "Now where was I? Despairing for his kingdom, Alfred prayed to his ancestors, said to include the ancient god Woden, for help. According to the legend, his plea was answered, and when he led his army out of the marshes and joined the battle once more, he was now possessed of superhuman powers. He drove the Viking hordes back into the sea and became the first king of what we now call England, and the first Defender of the Realm. After he died, his powers lived on, transferring from monarch to monarch, and now they have reached you."

"What powers? What can I do?"

"Come back to the Keep tomorrow and we'll show you."

- THIRTEEN -

The Real
Crown Jewels

"Ow!" Alfie protested.

"Ah, come on, that didn't hurt," barked Brian as he took another swipe at Alfie with a wooden sword. "Fight back!"

"Ow!"

They were in the Arena, a large oval-shaped dirt floor, fringed by plain benches on one side and a purple velvet curtain on the other, set beneath a tall, dark tower. There were heavy leather dummies on stands, swinging chains with cannonballs tied to the end of them, and even a quintain—a sandbag dangling from a pole used for jousting practice. It was like a medieval boxing gym.

"Why are there so many fire extinguishers?" Alfie had asked when Brian first ushered him in from the Map Room. There were indeed more than a normal number lining one wall of the Arena.

"Different ones for different types of flame,"

said Brian. "Don't worry about it; we probably won't even set you on fire till tomorrow."

Alfie was wearing cricket pads on his legs, and a helmet, but they weren't doing much to deflect the blows from Brian, mainly because the gleeful trainer kept aiming for parts of Alfie's body that weren't protected.

Alfie threw down his wooden sword and stepped away. "Ow! Why do THEY have to watch?"

A gaggle of beefeaters were sitting on the benches drinking tea and eating scones piled with strawberry jam and cream.

"Tea break, Majesty," said Seabrook, the white-bearded new chief yeoman warder. Alfie was pretty sure he heard some snickering at the back of the group.

The Lord Chamberlain looked up from behind his newspaper and scowled at the beefeaters, who took the hint and bustled out of the Arena, back to their desks.

"So is this it?" asked Alfie. "I thought you were going to show me what I could do. You know, *powers* . . ."

"Tsch, kids today, they want everything handed to them on a plate," sighed Brian.

"Come now, king's armorer, stop teasing His Majesty," said LC. "We really do need to get on with things."

Muttering under his breath, Brian marched over to the tall velvet curtains and pulled a thick rope. The curtains parted to reveal a tapestry of a rather plump-looking Defender doing battle with a six-headed Hydra, each head seeming to bear the face of a different woman. Alfie was startled to see Brian grab on to the fat king's codpiece and twist it hard to the side. The picture split in two and slid apart to reveal an enormous glass case, framed in heavy oak. Inside was a glittering array of ornately made weapons and jewels: crowns, swords, scepters, bracelets, spurs, and a ring. Alfie recognized them at once. "The Crown Jewels. But I thought they were kept upstairs?"

"That pile of junk?" said Brian. "That's just for the tourists."

"These are the Regalia, your Majesty," added LC. "The *real* Crown Jewels. Look closer."

Alfie leaned in and peered through the glass. At once the items nearest to him began to glow with a strange golden light. Alfie recoiled in shock, then leaned in again, and once more the surface of the swords, crowns, and other treasures shimmered.

"They can tell you are near," said LC.

"Me?" said Alfie.

Brian elbowed Alfie aside and opened a drawer beneath the display case. "All right, enough yakking, you two. Time to do some work. Lose your clothes and put this on."

Brian pulled out a thin, faded-white linen sleeveless shirt with frilly edges. It didn't look like it had been cleaned for about a hundred years—the only thing that looked new about it was the gold stitching that had repaired a long, blue-stained tear in the chest.

"You want me to put that on?" asked Alfie, wondering if it was a joke.

"This is the *Colobium sindonis*, Your Majesty," said LC. "Otherwise known as the Shroud Tunic. It has been worn by every British monarch, all the way back to King Alfred the Great himself. It is the most precious of the ancient regalia."

"It looks like a nightie."

"Yes, I suppose it does a bit."

Brian and LC were staring at him, and he got the distinct impression they were not going to stop staring until he did as they asked. So he reluctantly removed his shirt and trousers and pulled the old tunic over his head. It smelled musty, like something you might find in a charity shop, but at least it was nice and baggy—

Alfie gasped as he felt all the air sucked from his lungs. The tunic clung to his body as if it were alive, pulsating and growing over his chest, back, arms, and legs. Alfie screamed as the writhing material crawled up his neck and over his head and face. For a moment there was complete darkness. Then he realized he still had his eyes screwed shut.

"Take a look, Majesty."

Alfie open his eyes and was relieved to find that he could still see, though there was a slight sheen to the Arena around him, as if he were looking through highly polished glass. Brian wheeled a full-length mirror over to him. In it, Alfie could see himself—but not himself. Where he had been standing a moment before, shivering in his boxer shorts, there was now a noble-looking white knight. But not a knight in some clunky medieval armor; rather, his suit seemed to be formed from a single piece of mysterious, flexible metal alloy, bending without resistance as he gingerly moved his arms up and down and bent his knees. It was so light that if he hadn't been able to see himself in the mirror, Alfie would have sworn he wasn't wearing anything at all. The helmet was sleek, with only the slight impression of eye cavities and a mouth slit. His face was completely concealed, yet the air inside here smelled better than the cleanest seaside breeze. He had seen this knight, this stranger standing before him, in countless blurry photos and video clips over the years, but now here he was. It was as if he had stepped into someone else's skin.

"I'm . . . the Defender."

"That's the spirit, sir," said LC, patting him on the back. "Carry on, Brian!"

The Lord Chamberlain stalked back to the benches and returned to his newspaper.

Alfie turned just in time to see Brian heaving a bowling ball through the air at his face. On reflex, Alfie put his hands up. But as the heavy ball collided with his fist, it split in two and fell away in a cloud of dust.

"Whoa."

"You need to stop thinking and start moving!" shouted Brian as he readied his next missile—a fence post wrapped in barbed wire. Alfie couldn't help jumping away as Brian hurled it at his legs. But he was amazed to find that as he landed back on the post, it crumbled under his boot. He kicked what remained of it away, and it spun twenty feet and smashed against a wall.

"OK. *That* was cool."

The Defender's armor made Alfie feel ten times taller and faster. He was actually strong for the first time in his life. He'd have loved to give it a go on the rugby field at school; he'd be unstoppable, scattering people everywhere and making a beeline for that thug Mortimer.

"It feels like I could run through a brick wall!"

"Of course you could," replied Brian.

"But please don't," interjected LC, glancing up from his paper. "At least, not down here. The foundations aren't what they used to be."

Alfie clenched his fists—he could feel the power of the armor buzzing around him. "What makes it tick?"

"You do, sir," said the Lord Chamberlain. "It is the same for all the Crown Jewels—only you can make them work."

Brian opened the glass case and pulled out the largest sword, offering it to Alfie. "Let's try out the Great Sword of State, shall we?"

Alfie took it in his gloved hand. He was expecting it to feel heavy, but it was lighter than a tennis racquet. He gripped the jewel-encrusted hilt with its sculpted gold cross guards, one in the shape of a lion, the other a unicorn, and prepared to pull the sword from its sheath.

"Wait a second!" said Brian.

He put on a pair of Ray-Ban aviator sunglasses, while LC pulled a pair of old-fashioned green glass goggles over his eyes.

Alfie unsheathed the sword and it exploded into light, the steel blade radiating a blinding glare that illuminated the entire Arena before settling down into a steady glow. Alfie swayed the blade back and forth. Like his magical armor, it was light and comfortable, almost as if . . . as if it were made especially for him.

Brian looked on proudly. "That blade is Damascus steel, finest in the world. Enchanted, of course. It'll cut a car in half."

Alfie laughed. "Yeah, right."

Brian pulled a lever, and with a clank of chains and a deep rumble, a battered old scrapyard car rose through the floor on a stone dais. "Go ahead if you don't believe me."

Alfie gawked. "You seriously want me to cut a car in half?"

Brian smiled and patted Alfie on the back playfully. "No, just kidding."

Inside his helmet, Alfie smiled, relieved.

"OF COURSE I WANT YOU TO CUT IT IN HALF, YOU LITTLE WEED!" yelled the armorer. He slapped Alfie on the side of the head for good measure, and although it didn't hurt, it still shocked him.

"You will not call His Majesty a weed!" snapped LC.

Brian ignored the old man, grabbed Alfie by his now-massive steel shoulders, and went nose to nose with him. "YOU'RE DEFENDER OF THE REALM! WHAT ARE YOU GOING TO DO WHEN YOU FACE OFF WITH A

NORWEGIAN BOG TROLL OR A SIBERIAN BEAR-MAN! ASK THEM TO TEA?! NOW GET SWINGING!"

Alfie looked at the car and the glowing, pulsing sword in his hand. He shrugged, swung the sword over his head, and brought it down with a shower of sparks and ripping metal. The two separate pieces of the car spun around and, once they had come to a stop and his amazement had passed, Alfie put his foot on the hood like a hunter posing with a trophy.

LC clapped politely. "You cut a Nissan Micra right in half! Well done, sir!"

Nonchalant, Alfie spun the Great Sword around and tried to slide it back into its sheath—but couldn't do it. "Um . . . Brian, can you give me a hand?"

The training went on all morning, as Brian gave Alfie a demonstration of some of the other powers of the real Crown Jewels. There was the Sword of Mercy, with its blunted square tip, so called because it was only to be drawn "in mercy, not in vengeance." Touched on the shoulder of someone wounded, it could heal them in an instant, if applied soon enough. There was the Orb, a golden sphere topped with a cross, which Alfie could hang from his belt along with his sword. It was nicknamed the "Scout Orb" because when Alfie released it, it flew on ahead of him, giving him a view in his mind's eye of whatever lay around the next corner. It was a strange sensation, as if he were watching the world through someone else's eyes, and he struggled to get the hang of it.

"Takes a little practice, that one," remarked Brian. "Handy, though, if you want to avoid blundering into an ambush."

There were the Spurs, which locked on to his boots seamlessly. LC told him that they housed Wyvern, the Defender's horse, who could be summoned by saying, or merely thinking, the word *spurs*. But they decided not to bother her today, as she was still feeling a little emotional after King Henry's death. Alfie thought that sounded ominous.

Next, there was a little golden spoon. Alfie had snorted with laughter at that one. "Let me guess, this gives me the power to eat yogurt really, really fast?"

LC and Brian were stony faced.

Alfie frowned. "Boiled eggs?"

LC whipped it out of his hand, telling him that it was in fact the seven-hundred-year-old Anointing Spoon for dispensing sacred oil and ingesting potions.

But Alfie was having fun now—he felt like he'd been given the keys to the best toy shop in the world. He picked out the only item that was left—the ring. To call it bling would be to seriously undersell it: a cross of red rubies laid against a bed of blue sapphires, circled by dozens of finely cut diamonds. It reminded him of the national flag, the Union Jack, which seemed apt. But unlike the other regalia, this one did not glow at all when Alfie held it.

"Is it broken?" Alfie asked.

Brian hurried over and took the ring from his hand, placing it back into its velvet housing as carefully as if he were handling a live grenade.

"No, it's not *broken*, you cheeky brat."

"What does it do? Shoot laser beams? Make me invisible? Ooh—does it mean I can teleport to wherever I want to go?! That would be epic."

"No, Majesty," said LC with all the patience he could muster. "The ring harnesses your ability to command all things born of British soil."

"What, like plants?" said Alfie, disappointed.

"Plants and trees, yes, you could use it on those, I imagine," LC continued. "But much more than that. Look around you, sir. The stone that makes these walls, the metal that supports them, all of it was mined from the earth of this great country. Your connection with the land and fabric of your kingdom runs deep; it is an ancient bond, which you can learn to control."

Alfie thought about the pen that had shot

through the sofa into his hand in his dad's study; the doors that had flown open in the Tower on his first visit.

"Made in the United Kingdom! I've done it before . . ."

"The power can leak out under moments of high stress," explained LC. "But this is one ability that will not be yours to master until after the Succession has been permanently locked in by the sacred rites of the coronation. That is why the ring does not yet respond to you."

Superhero armor. Magic swords. Mysterious powers. This could take some getting used to. And he hadn't even had lunch yet. Brian showed Alfie how to remove his armor. As it turned out, it was easy. Alfie just had to reach up, as he would to take off a shirt, and the hard shell melted away, leaving nothing but the Shroud Tunic once more. Brian took it from him and put it back in its drawer beneath the Regalia Cabinet.

"So that's what it feels like . . . To be a hero, I mean," said Alfie.

Brian guffawed. "Don't let it go to your head, matey."

"Thank you, Brian," said LC as he steered Alfie out into the Map Room.

"That's what the Defender is, though, isn't it?" asked Alfie as they strolled under the tapestries, each depicting a different Defender from past centuries. "A superhero?"

"Some Defenders have been great and noble heroes, no doubt," said LC. "Take Harold the Third, for example—he didn't just visit bomb sites during the war; he took out a fair few enemy planes himself. Although he spent more time tackling the high-altitude pterodactyl squadrons."

Alfie opened his mouth to ask about a hundred different questions, then thought better of it.

"Here's Elizabeth the First," continued LC. "She personally defended our shores from the Spanish king and his armada of vampire mermaids . . . And there's brave Henry the Fifth—he led his army to victory over the French king's centaur cavalry."

Alfie laughed, wondering what Professor Lock would make of this kind of history lesson.

"You wouldn't have laughed if you were there, believe me, sir," said LC. "Not every monarch has made a good Defender, of course . . ."

LC pulled a lever, and Alfie was startled to see the tapestries swivel around, replaced by new ones depicting different Defenders, each of them engaged in much less noble, more villainous deeds. "We call this our wall of shame."

A throaty "BOO!" rose up from the beefeaters' desks, finished off by a ripple of low chuckling.

"Feckless King John used to fly around drunk, starting fights with giants," continued LC. "Mary the First—'Bloody Mary' they called her—liked to pluck her enemies from their beds before burning them at the stake. That's Richard the Third—he made a deal with a witch to help him murder his own nephews. Well, it was either him or Henry the Seventh—it's a murky period, that one."

Alfie was pleased to see that not all his predecessors were perfect. "I guess my family has had its fair share of bad apples, same as any other."

"Indeed, Majesty. You may be the Defender of the Realm, but whether you will be a hero . . . well, let's just say the jury is out. Right, then, back to your training, I think, sir?"

Alfie flexed his aching limbs and trudged after LC, back into the Arena.

FOURTEEN

There's Something in the Water

"Glasses, Hayley! I need my glasses! The race is about to start!"

Hayley hauled a stuffed suitcase along the hall and deposited it with a pile of other bags by the front door. "On top of your head, Gran, just like last time."

Hayley's gran laughed as she put them on. "Silly old me. What would I do without you, eh?"

Hayley watched her gran turn the TV up far too loud for the third time that morning. Two teams of university rowers, one in light blue, the other dark blue, were climbing into their boats and readying their oars. The cameras cut to the thousands of spectators lining the river Thames. Hayley couldn't imagine why Gran was so excited about watching the boat race. She thought any race that only ever involved one of two teams winning sounded pretty pointless. Why not just toss a coin? But it was another "great British institution," and if it kept her gran happy a little while longer, then fine. Happiness was going to be in short supply for them both by the end of the day.

Hayley thought she'd been pretty smart to call the police when the two rogue agents turned up. What she hadn't thought about was all the attention it would get them afterward. A friendly policewoman who had helped them tidy up the mess had clocked Gran's shaky mental state; Gran kept calling for Lawrence to stop being such a "Lazy Larry" and come help them, until Hayley had to explain who she was talking about. The policewoman asked Hayley how old she was, and as soon as she answered truthfully, she knew she'd sealed their fate.

The next few days were taken up with meeting after phone call after more meetings with social workers. Finally, they issued both Hayley and her gran with an emergency care order. Gran would be placed in an old people's home and Hayley would go into foster care. When they first told her, Hayley had shouted and screamed and cried. But her main social worker, Sandra, had patiently explained that it didn't mean she couldn't see her gran anymore—she could visit her every day if she wanted to. They just needed to make sure that she was looked after. Hayley could now spend more time being a teenager and less time being a full-time caregiver. It sounded fair enough, but Hayley still cried herself to sleep that night.

What settled it for Hayley in the end was the realization that maybe this way they would be safe from the two brutes who were after the lizard scale—though, of course, she didn't tell Sandra that.

Hayley had been keeping a constant lookout, in case the scary pair decided to return. A screech of tires outside last night had sent her rushing to the window, but it was just that idiot Dean Barron and his mates pulling hand-brake turns in his vomit-colored car. Maybe they wouldn't come back at all? Or maybe they were just waiting for the stream of visitors from social services to die down so they could make their move? Either way, it was probably safest to go. It would be strange leaving the place where she'd grown up, but perhaps it was time.

Hayley had tried to explain to her gran what was going to happen, but Gran had gotten it into her head that they were moving to a hotel while the city council finally redecorated the flat. Hayley figured it wasn't a bad thing for her to believe right now, so she'd stopped correcting her.

Suddenly, Hayley's gran gasped and dropped her mug of tea. Hayley rushed over to make sure she hadn't scalded herself. "Gran! Are you all right?"

The old woman was pointing at the TV with a shaking finger. "Did you see that?"

Hayley turned her attention to the screen. There was some sort of commotion on the river. The two boats seemed to have capsized, and the rowers were splashing around in the water. Hayley couldn't help laughing—this was much more entertaining than some boring race. But her gran shushed her and turned up the volume further. The commentator was breathless: "Something's happened, we're not sure—there seemed to be a freak wave and, yes, here's the replay now . . ."

The footage showed a huge wall of water surging downriver, spectators screaming and pointing, then the confusion of the impact, the boats flipping over. And just under the water's surface, a large, dark object, moving with the wave.

"What's that?" asked Hayley.

The commentator stuttered on: "It looks like . . . there's something in the water. It's difficult to make it out . . . it's headed for the bridge."

• • •

Alfie was perched on a stool in the Arena sipping tea and chomping his way through another round of toast when the alarm sounded. LC and Brian exchanged a worried glance and hurried out to the Map Room, Alfie close behind them.

Beefeaters were crowded around the ops table. A small light was flashing on the edge of London. The chief yeoman warder was on the phone—he put his hand over the receiver and addressed the Lord Chamberlain.

"It's the Southwark burgh. There's been an activity spike. Waiting for visual confirmation."

"Anything on the wires?" asked LC.

Beefeaters scurried back and forth, turning on radios and old televisions, skipping through frequencies and channels.

"What's going on?" Alfie asked.

Brian moved him aside. "They've detected supernatural activity—but it's very unusual this near the city center; probably a false alarm. Just keep out of the way."

A beefeater wheeled a television over to them. "You should see this!"

Alfie pushed his way through the scrum of bodies until he could see the screen. The TV was tuned in to the coverage of the boat race. Hundreds of spectators were running from one side of Hammersmith Bridge to the other as a long black shape streaked underneath, splashing water high onto the granite of the suspension towers. The tip of a dark, scaly, spike-covered tail broke the surface for a moment, and the creature turned, churning the dirty river water and heading back the way it had come, before going deeper and disappearing.

"The Black Lizard. It's back." LC's voice was tight with concern.

Rescue boats were starting to reach the rowers, who were treading water in the middle of the river. Along the shoreline, calm was just descending over the spectators once more when suddenly there was a rushing sound, like a bath beginning to drain. The entire river current seemed to stop, and the surface began to turn, pulling the boats and stranded rowers around in a huge circle. A giant whirlpool was forming.

Alfie was frozen, a single thought pulsing through his brain. *Ellie.* Hadn't she told him she was going to the boat race? He fumbled for his phone—he could just about get a signal down here—and dialed her number. When she answered, there was something in her voice he had never heard before: fear.

"Ellie? Is that you? Where are you?"

"I'm on the bridge! Are you seeing this, Alfie?"

Alfie looked back to the television just in time to see thick white lines shoot out from the spiraling vortex of water like torpedoes toward the shore. He gasped as shock waves smashed into the riverbank, throwing people off their feet, cracking the sidewalk, and shattering windows. Two more torpedo lines burst from the whirlpool—and this time they were heading toward the bridge.

"LOOK OUT, ELLIE!" Alfie shouted into the phone.

The bridge bucked and rolled under the impact. Metal groaned and concrete cracked, falling into the river below, and screams rose from the hundreds of people standing along the bridge. Panic broke out.

Alfie yelled into the phone. "ELLIE? ELLIE?" But the line was dead. He threw his phone down and grabbed Brian. "Ellie's there—she's on the bridge!"

The Lord Chamberlain and Brian exchanged a grave look. "Don't worry, Majesty. I'm sure her security detail will deal with the situation," said LC.

"You didn't hear her! She's in trouble! We have to do something!" shouted Alfie.

"I'll call in, see if they've evacuated her," said Brian.

They turned their backs to him and consulted with the beefeaters who were working the phones. Alfie looked back at the TV screen and frantically scanned the mass of bodies fighting to flee the bridge—if Ellie was in the middle of that, there was no way they would be able to pull her out. Another huge chunk of concrete broke off from the bridge and splashed into the river below. There was no time to wait. Alfie had to help his sister. Right now. He sprinted back into the Arena, pulled open the Regalia Cabinet, and grabbed the Shroud Tunic. He slipped it over his head and the Defender's magical armor spread across his body, the transformation complete in a second.

LC and Brian burst into the hall behind him.

"What do you think you're playing at?!" barked Brian.

"Saving my sister!" Alfie replied as he searched the cabinet of Crown Jewels.

"No, Majesty! You're not even close to being ready!" LC spluttered.

Alfie found what he was looking for: the Spurs. He could feel restless energy buzzing off them, like an impatient dog straining at its lead. The Spurs flew out of his hands and attached themselves with a satisfying *clunk* to his armored boots, like metal finding a powerful magnet. LC and Brian backed away, suddenly wary.

"OK, Alf, take the armor off, nice and slow." Brian's voice was low and calm. "Don't even think about saying the magic word."

"What, you mean *spurs?*" asked Alfie.

He'd barely finished saying it when the spectral horse exploded from his heels and dragged Alfie into the air so fast that he couldn't even catch his breath. The walls were a blur as Wyvern, whinnying indignantly, streaked around the Arena, buzzing over the benches and sending Brian and LC diving for cover. Alfie clawed the air, trying to find the reins, but Wyvern was flying too fast.

Alfie was just thinking *I hope this thing knows where the exit is!* when the ceiling high above the Arena spiraled open to reveal a rough-hewn vertical tunnel, and beyond, the sky. The horse rocketed upward and out through the roof.

The Lord Chamberlain and Brian looked up in astonishment.

"Maybe he's more ready than you think," said Brian.

Anyone watching the skies over the Tower of London at that precise moment might have thought they'd seen a flash of light shoot from the roof for a split second before disappearing. They would have been too far away to hear Alfie's desperate yells for the crazy flying horse to:

"STOP! SLOW DOWN! HEEL!"

But this wild creature—ghost, spirit animal, whatever she was—was clearly not in a listening mood. It wasn't just that Wyvern was fast (and she was: jet-plane-g-force-turning-your-face-into-a-wobbling-freak-show fast), it was that she was also bucking and twisting, even barrel-rolling, as she tried to throw Alfie off her back. He couldn't help feeling all of this was pretty unfair. *What have I done to upset her? I'm the Defender, aren't I?*

Alfie had never liked riding horses, but he knew enough to make a grab for the reins and pull on them as hard as he could. "The river! Get me to the river!" he shouted at the horse.

Wyvern shot up into a neck-breaking climb, and Alfie just hung on, hoping that he would get to Ellie in time, and that his arms and legs wouldn't pop out of their sockets before he arrived.

• • •

Ellie had arrived early to get a good spot right in the middle of the bridge. Now she wished she was watching on TV instead. She had dropped her phone into the water as the first shock waves hit. The screams were deafening as people pulled themselves to their feet and surged down the bridge, desperate to escape. Ellie looked around for Rhona, her royal protection officer, and saw her being pulled away in the tide of bodies scrambling to escape.

BOOM. The bridge shook beneath her feet. *BOOM. BOOM. BOOM.* The entire surface of the river seemed to jump as if someone had tossed a truckload of dynamite into it. A golden coat of arms tumbled from the top of the farthest bridge tower, smashing down in a shower of masonry. *SNAP.* A thick suspension cable came loose and danced like a broken guitar string over the steel rails. An ominous groan came from the bridge as it swayed drunkenly. The railing that Ellie was gripping cracked and arched away from her out over the river. Now there was nothing stopping her from sliding into the water a hundred feet below, save for her fingernails, which she dug into the fracturing tarmac.

Suddenly she heard a girl cry out nearby, "HELP ME!"

It took her a few moments to see where the voice was coming from. She craned her neck over the side of the bridge and spotted a green blazer— her school's uniform. It was a younger student she recognized, clinging on to a strut below the boardwalk. She must have tumbled through when the railings snapped. Her eyes were wide with shock and her face was ghostly white.

"HELP! HELP!"

"HOLD ON! I'M COMING!" Ellie shouted to the girl.

Time to make use of all that gym practice, thought Ellie as she swung herself off the side of the bridge and onto the steel strut below. The younger girl was lying across it, about ten feet away, shaking. *It's just like the balance beam, no big deal,* Ellie told herself. Except she couldn't help adding, *Yeah, apart from the hundred-foot drop and collapsing bridge part . . .* She focused on her target, extended her arms, and placed one foot in front of the other. Five steps in and the bridge started to shake so hard that planks bounced loose, plummeting past on either side. Ellie picked up the pace, and six steps later she made it. She grabbed the trembling girl and looked for a way they could both climb back up.

"ELEANOR! ELEANOR!"

It was her bodyguard, Rhona. She was right above them on the bridge.

"DOWN HERE!" cried Ellie.

The boardwalk peeled back and there was Rhona's bloodied, dirty face a few feet above them. "GIVE ME YOUR HAND!"

But Ellie lifted the younger girl first. "TAKE HER!"

Rhona grabbed hold of the girl's arms and hauled her up through the gap. The bodyguard's face appeared back at the hole, and Ellie reached up.

As she did so, the bridge lurched to the side, sending her sliding back down the length of the beam. Ellie clung on, like a cat stuck in a storm-blown tree, watching with horror as the main bridge towers disintegrated on either side of her. The structure let out a long, low whine, like the cry of a mortally wounded animal. It was going down.

On the walkway, Rhona had no choice but to scoop up the young girl and run for all she was worth back to the road. She made it just before the bridge gave way completely. As the strut Ellie was clinging to started to tumble, she pushed off as hard as she could, trying to clear the debris field and hoping that she'd find clear water at the end of this, the longest dive she'd ever attempted.

Ellie hit the water hard, arms first, at enough of an angle to stop her from being killed outright, but not enough to keep from being knocked unconscious.

She slipped beneath the surface.

High above, skirting the underside of a cloud on Wyvern, Alfie saw the bridge collapse. Below, the river was a scene of chaos as rowers swam around, clinging to wreckage.

But there was no sign of Ellie. He was too late. Tears streamed down his face underneath the helmet. The Black Lizard had killed his father and now it had taken his sister as well. "Ellie!" he sobbed.

Wyvern suddenly dived toward the river, tucking her legs up beneath her like a falcon streamlining its wings. Alfie screamed as they hit the water at supersonic speed, a white blur disappearing so fast into the depths that Alfie didn't even have time to hold his breath. The murky water was churning like a washing machine on spin cycle. Chunks of metal and wood tumbled past and clanged off his armor. Alfie, amazed that he could breathe underwater, struggled to get his bearings. Above them, he could just see the kicking feet of rowers treading water. But Wyvern seemed to know where she was going, swimming deeper, searching.

"That's it . . . find her, find her!" Alfie shouted. He pushed a large chunk of broken wood out of the way and peered through the gloom. A body plummeted past them, down to the bottom of the river, hair floating free. "Ellie!"

Wyvern was moving before Alfie even touched the reins, and the horse tucked its neck under Ellie's inert body and flicked her upward like a cork. She shot up and burst through the surface, spluttering awake, coughing up dirty water, very much alive. Alfie watched from below as the underside of a rescue boat glided to his sister's side. He could hear the deep throb of the engine and muffled shouts as hands reached over and pulled his sister out of the river.

"That's it, Wyvern! Yes!" Alfie slapped her shoulder, but she tried to bite him. "Hey! I'm trying to be nice."

Too late, Alfie caught a glance of something else snaking its way through the water toward him. He could make out scaly, black limbs; a thick, spiked tail; and long, razor-toothed jaws. The Black Lizard.

The creature circled Alfie impatiently, changing directions, fixing him with its devilish red eyes, like it was mightily annoyed that the Defender had crashed its party on the river.

In a panic, Alfie reached for his sword, but remembered that in his rush to leave the Tower he hadn't taken it. He was a sitting duck. Alfie braced himself, praying his armor or Wyvern might save him . . . but the Black Lizard abruptly turned away, as if deciding he wasn't worth the trouble. With one pump of its wide tail, it disappeared into the deep—the powerful wake rocking Alfie back in his saddle.

- FIFTEEN -

The Shrine
of the Confessor

"I was SO close to telling her. So close!"

Alfie was sitting in the backseat of a Range
Rover next to LC as Brian swerved through traffic.
They had just visited Ellie in the hospital. Incredibly
she had nothing more than a few bruises from her
experience. She was more embarrassed at all the
fuss everyone was making—the media was calling her the "Hero Princess" for rescuing the young
girl on the bridge.

Alfie had perched at the end of her hospital bed
and somehow managed not to tell her that he'd
flown over on a magic horse and saved her from
drowning. He was still buzzing from his first out-
ing as the Defender—unlike LC, whose face was
like thunder.

"I'm rather pleased you didn't, sir. That was by
far the most irresponsible, downright foolish thing
I have *ever* seen."

"What was I supposed to do? Let her drown? I saved her, didn't I?"

"I rather think it was Wyvern who did all the saving," LC sniffed.

Ouch, Alfie thought as he looked out the window and felt his good mood leaking away. It was true. Not that he was going to admit that to LC. He tuned back in to the old man's rant.

". . . and thirdly, absolutely anything could have happened out there. You could have been spotted, and then where would we be?"

Alfie thought about it. "How many people know who the Defender really is?"

"The chief yeoman warder, the thirty-seven yeoman warders, and myself and Brian, naturally," said the Lord Chamberlain.

"Not the police?"

"No, Majesty."

"The army?"

"No, sir."

"The prime minister?"

Brian laughed and slapped the steering wheel. "Might as well call the papers yourself!"

"The internal security services, MI5 and so on, have been an interested party for years now," said LC. "They know the Defender is real and they'd certainly *like* to know who he is."

"Aren't we kind of on the same side, though? Protecting Britain?" Alfie asked.

"Technically, yes. But MI5 doesn't take kindly to freelancers."

Alfie turned it all over in his head. Forty-one people in all who knew about the Defender. It sounded like a lot. All it took was one blabbermouth to blow the whole thing wide open.

"So what's stopping one of the beefeaters—sorry, yeoman warders—from saying something?"

"Ah, well, sir, we have a secret weapon for that," said LC.

"Cool. What is it?" asked Alfie. "A potion that stops them from talking? Or, like a laser beam that erases their memories?"

"No. It's a little something called *loyalty*." The old man practically growled the word. "The yeoman warders have been the monarch's steadfast bodyguards for over five hundred years, and they have always kept their silence. Believe me, if the population at large ever found out about all the foul creatures that threaten these shores, there would be mass panic."

Alfie shuddered. "Like this Black Lizard thing, you mean? Oh, it's got a tail now, by the way."

The Lord Chamberlain frowned as he gazed out at the pedestrians watching the passing motorcade.

"It is changing, becoming more powerful. So far it has struck the Tower, Stonehenge, and under the Thames. It's as if it is searching for something."

"I lost my contact lenses once. Turned the place upside down, made a real mess," said Alfie. But LC's face was stern. "Yeah, it's not really the same," Alfie added.

"The problem is, he's a crafty so-and-so," barked Brian from the front. "It's not like he's even left us any clues to go on."

Clues. Something was nagging at Alfie— something he'd seen. The car drew to a halt outside the western entrance of Westminster Abbey, and Brian leapt out to open the door. They were here to attend a rehearsal for the coronation that was due to happen in two short weeks' time. The church's two great towers loomed over Alfie as he climbed out and straightened his tie (how he hated ties). He made his way toward the reception committee, a huddle of priests who were bent under their umbrellas. A gray-haired bishop dropped a prayer book and was just bending down to pick it up when a thought struck Alfie. A memory. He stopped and turned back to LC.

"There is a clue! Ellie sent me a video clip of that night at the Tower. It was online."

LC looked blank. He probably thought "online" meant something to do with hanging his underwear out to dry. Alfie fished out his phone, found Ellie's email, and clicked on the attachment. LC and Brian studied the shaky footage of the Defender and the Black Lizard fighting at the Tower in front of the Jewel House.

"Yes, yes, we know all this—the yeoman warders gave us a full report," whispered LC. The priests were peering over at them, puzzled.

"Wait," said Alfie, "it's at the end."

They kept watching until the moment when the Defender sliced off one of the lizard's scales. It flew off, landed in the old woman's wheelchair, and was picked up by the girl who was with her.

The two men exchanged a hopeful look. "Find her," LC ordered Brian.

Before Alfie could protest, Brian snatched the phone out of his hands, jumped back in the Range Rover, and roared away.

LC ushered Alfie toward the Abbey. "Very well, sir, back to the day job. Big smile. Just pretend you're normal."

Alfie plastered on a fake grin. "I'll do my best."

• • •

Alfie had been inside Westminster Abbey many times before—for weddings, Remembrance Day services, and his father's funeral, of course— but somehow this time was different. This time the ancient church was being prepared for a coronation—for *his* coronation. The idea was suddenly overwhelming. The great vaulted ceiling felt even higher and more breathtaking than usual; every monument, memorial, and statue seemed to cast a shadow over him. The names and faces of the country's most famous rulers, soldiers, scientists, and artists pressed in from all sides, daring him to pretend he was worthy to stand among them. He knew that he wasn't.

"Just think of it as a play, Alfie." Professor Lock stepped out from behind King Edward's Chair, a surprisingly battered-looking, plain wooden throne, on which the monarch sat to be crowned. Alfie smiled. It was a relief to see a friendly face.

The Lord Chamberlain nodded a stiff greeting to the teacher. "We felt that Your *Majesty* might benefit from some extra historical tutelage before the ceremony." Alfie noticed LC's emphasis on "majesty"—he clearly did not approve of Lock's informal style. But for Alfie it was a welcome breath of fresh air.

"It's good to see you, sir," said Alfie. "How are things at the prison? I mean, school."

"We all very much miss your late-night escape attempts," said Lock with a wry smile.

"Has Mortimer broken his leg playing rugby yet?"

"Not that I know of."

"That's a shame." Alfie grinned. "What did you mean, a play?"

His teacher looked to the Lord Chamberlain, as if seeking permission to hold the floor. LC nodded and withdrew. Lock continued: "I know it feels like you're going to be under the spotlight, Alfie, but actually this whole thing isn't really about you at all. You're just a prop—a symbol—same as the robes and crowns and even this dusty old chair."

Alfie knew the professor was trying to make him feel better, but the idea of being "on stage" at all made his knees go weak. "I've never really done any acting."

"Oh, come on, Alfie," laughed Lock. "I've seen you waving at the crowds and smiling. Oscar-winning stuff! Anyway, that's what rehearsals are for. So, shall we?"

Lock proceeded to guide Alfie through the bizarre sequence of rituals that would make up the coronation ceremony. It was like being back at school, watching his teacher bring to life some chapter from a history textbook, with his easy charisma and boundless knowledge. Even the wizened old Dean of Westminster, who would be leading the service on the day, along with his retinue of clerics and helpers, seemed spellbound by the young professor's performance.

Lock explained that, like a play, the ceremony

had a bunch of different "acts." They all had very grand names like "the Recognition," "the Oath," "the Crowning," but what they meant in practice was a lot of "face this way, hold this, say that" for Alfie to get his head around.

Next, Alfie had to practice the part of the coronation called "the Anointing."

"Now don't be alarmed, Your M-M-Majesty, but before we anoint you with the holy oil, my c-c-colleagues will be placing a c-c-canopy over your head." The Dean of Westminster's voice was as shaky as his hands. If he was the one anointing him with oil, then Alfie thought he had better bring a raincoat.

Professor Lock took over again, explaining that the Anointing would not even be filmed—it was considered too sacred, as it was the moment that the monarch's authority was supposedly conveyed by a higher power. Although, he told Alfie, these days everyone knew that the king only held the throne with permission from the people—they were willing to have a king, as long as that king didn't have any *real* power. Alfie thought he detected a hint of disappointment in his teacher's voice, like this was a sorry state of affairs.

But he also remembered what LC had already told him about this, the most special part of the ceremony—something that even Professor Lock couldn't possibly know—that the Anointing was when Alfie would fully become the Defender. It would be the moment that ended the turbulent Succession and sealed in the powers that had been swirling around him. How had LC put it? "It's when you become one with your destiny."

"My destiny," Alfie said out loud, without meaning to.

"Destiny?" replied Lock. "Yes, I suppose so, in fact . . ." Alfie followed Lock's gaze as he looked underneath King Edward's Chair, but there was nothing there. "Ah, of course, it must still be on the way here," said Lock. Seeing Alfie's puzzled expression, he explained: "On the day, there will be a large slab of red sandstone underneath your chair. The Stone of Destiny—that's just one of its names—is kept in Scotland, but no one really knows where it came from originally. It's figured in the coronation for centuries—but don't worry about that; it's not important."

Alfie's mind felt like it was going to burst, there was so much crammed into it now. If this was really just a play, then he hoped there would be an intermission. Lock sensed his student's exhaustion and suggested a break.

• • •

Alfie wandered alone through the dim Abbey, past countless tombs and silent, candlelit chapels. He'd been there all day, and the light coming through the stained-glass windows was fading. As he circled back to the other side of the High Altar, he found himself standing in front of a giant monument, tiered rectangular tombs stacked on top of one another like a stone wedding cake. It was ornately carved with gold arches and seemed very old. He wondered who was buried inside the cold stone. The thought made him jumpy. Whose idea was it to fill a place like this with dead bodies?

Professor Lock strolled past and spotted him gazing up at the huge tomb. "The shrine of Edward the Confessor. But you knew that, right?" he teased.

"Well, I guess he's some great ancestor of mine or something, so I probably should." Alfie tried to smile, but the darkness of this place was starting to get to him.

"Alfie, I never said how sorry I was about your father. I can only imagine how overwhelming all of this must be for you." Lock placed a comforting hand on Alfie's shoulder.

"Understatement of the year, sir. It's just with everyone telling me what I have to do the whole time, I feel like I'm being . . ." Alfie searched for the word, but couldn't find it.

". . . herded?" Lock asked.

It was uncanny how Lock seemed to be able to read his mind. "Sorry, I shouldn't whine about it. It's not like I have any choice," Alfie said.

Lock was looking at him, frowning with concern. Alfie could see that his teacher wanted to say something. "What is it, sir?"

"I'm not sure it's really my place to say, but . . . let me show you something."

Lock led him down an aisle toward another tomb. Two age-pitted statues were lying on top of a bed of black stone, their hands clasped in prayer for eternity.

"Richard the Second and his wife, Anne. In 1399 he did something that had never been done before. He abdicated the throne. Do you know what that means?"

"He gave it up?" Alfie guessed.

"Exactly. Some say he was forced to; others claim that he stepped aside. Poor old Dickie wasn't in the best of health and we historians are still arguing about whether it was for the best."

Lock leaned against the tomb and looked at Alfie. He checked the aisle to see if they were being overheard.

"My point is, no matter how backed into a corner you feel, there are always choices in life, even for you . . . 'It matters not how strait the gate, how charged with punishments the scroll, I am the

master of my fate, I am the captain of my soul.'"
Alfie's teacher smiled, kindly. "Do me a favor and
think about what that means."

Alfie nodded. "The captain of my soul. I like
that . . ."

Raised voices split the silence as the Lord
Chamberlain hurried toward them. "Excuse me,
Professor Lock. I'm afraid I need to borrow His
Majesty. Something urgent has come up."

"By all means." Professor Lock smiled, courte-
ous, but looked at Alfie. "We'll talk again, Alfie.
You're the captain, remember."

Frowning again at the professor's use of the
king's first name, the Lord Chamberlain ushered
Alfie down the aisle and out of the Abbey.

Outside, the evening was cool and damp. Brian
opened the door of the Range Rover and bundled
him inside. In seconds they were careering through
traffic. Alfie was annoyed and tired. All he wanted
was something to eat and then a solid eight hours
of sleep.

"What's the rush?"

"The girl in your video—her name is Hayley
Hicks," said Brian. "British citizen. Fourteen years
old. Lives on an estate in Watford. Problem is, we
aren't the only ones who know about her."

"What do you mean?" asked Alfie.

Brian accelerated through a red light as the

outriders blocked the side roads. "I got a tip-off from a mate in MI5. They've tracked her down and they're on their way to pick her up right now. If we're ever going to find out what that creature is and how we can defeat it, we need to get to her first and make her hand over the lizard's scale."

"Sounds like a plan," said Alfie, gripping his armrest. "But won't people wonder why we're driving off to some estate in Watford?"

LC, who had been fiddling nervously with his watch, finally piped up. "*We're* not going there, Majesty. *You* are. And you're not going by car . . ."

SIXTEEN

Rooftop Rescue

They're coming to take me away, ha, ha! They're coming to take me away, ho, ho!

The words from one of the old songs her gran used to sing around the house had been playing on a loop inside Hayley's head all morning. She was in her bedroom, shoving clothes into her backpack and trying not to cry. Sandra, her social worker, was due to arrive in an hour's time, to wrench her away from everything she knew.

Hayley was still half expecting Gran to call out for her—something about wanting another cup of tea or asking what time her favorite game show was on. But Hayley's gran was already gone. The nurses from the Whisper Grove Rest Home (seriously, who named these places?) had rocked up earlier that morning. Hayley felt bad that she hadn't been nicer to them; in fact, when one of them had said that it must be a relief to see her gran going to a place where they could look after her "properly," she'd told him to "shove his thick head down the loo." The nurse had looked shocked, so Hayley had tried to keep a lid on her anger after that. It wasn't their fault, she told herself. They were just doing their jobs.

As for her gran, she was having one of her funny turns and thought she was going on vacation and that they might miss the flight. "Hurry up, Lawrence! That's my suitcase! No, *that* one. You're like a man made of smoke."

The male nurse had become her long-dead husband and, actually, it was pretty funny to see him being ordered around. He'd played along with it, winking at Hayley. She could see the nurses knew what they were doing. And the fact that her gran didn't even want to say good-bye to her made it easier too: There wasn't time, since "the plane was about to leave without them!" It seemed to be all over in a flash. One minute Hayley and her gran shared a life together, and the next minute it had ended.

Hayley had stood outside watching the care-home ambulance drive away, feeling like someone had sucked all the air out of her. Tears streamed down her face. The sun was going down on the saddest day of her life. Then Dean Barron started his stupid puke-green car up across the road, filling the air with exhaust fumes, honking his horn at her and grinning sarcastically. So Hayley had retreated back inside to pack.

Knock, knock!

Hayley's heart sank as she checked her watch. Sandra was early. She walked to the front door and peered through the peephole. Adrenaline shot through her body like a lightning bolt. It wasn't the social worker outside. It was the dead-eyed little man and his towering hulk-woman partner. Hayley kicked herself for dropping her guard. There had been no sign of the fake detectives since they first came by, and she'd let herself think they'd lost interest in her. But here they were. She had only a few seconds to make a plan.

The man put his eye to the other side of the peephole.

"Peekaboo, Hayley!" said Turpin. "We thought you might be lonely."

Fulcher nudged him aside and flexed her muscles. "Enough small talk, eh?" She thumped a size-twelve boot into the door and the lock snapped like a twig.

There was no sign of Hayley in the hall. Fulcher smacked every door open one by one, while Turpin followed close behind, scanning all the usual hiding places. He calculated that in an apartment this small it would take less than ten seconds to locate their prey.

Fulcher came out of the main bedroom looking puzzled. She shrugged. Turpin pushed past her, irritated. "She must be here somewhere!"

The bedroom was empty. The door to the small balcony was open, but Hayley was nowhere to be seen. He was about to leave the room when he noticed a thin red cord, tied around the grandmother's handrail at the side of the bed. He followed it across the floor and out onto the balcony, where it disappeared over the wall. Curious, he leaned over and saw Hayley swinging from the end of the cord below him.

"SHE'S HERE, YOU FOOL!" yelled Turpin.

Fulcher came running. She grabbed the red cord and yanked on it hard, pulling it back into the room.

Dangling under the window, fourteen floors above the ground, Hayley screamed. Her toe had just touched the top of the balcony wall of the apartment below when she heard Turpin's yell and felt the cord hoisting her back up. There was no choice. Either she let go now and hoped she'd land on her target or they were going to snatch her. Hayley swung herself as close to the tower-block wall as she could and jumped.

Her feet hit the top of the balcony below, skidding toward the edge. But she kept her balance and hopped off. She dashed into the flat and past an astonished old man—Mr. Pollard, who had lived below her and her gran for years.

"Sorry, Mr. P!"

"No problem, Hayley," he replied. "How's your gran?"

"Fine, thanks!" she shouted as she hurtled down the hall and out of the apartment.

Meanwhile Fulcher lay on her back, cursing. Turpin scrambled past her. "GET UP, YOU GREAT LUNK!"

Hayley hit the stairwell at full speed. She was confident she could outrun them in a straight chase, but she needed to get out of the tower block first. However, instead of heading down the staircase, she went up. She had to collect the lizard's scale. If she left without it, then none of this would have been worth it.

Stopping one floor above her own, Hayley whipped off her hoodie and knotted it around the door handles to the stairwell, tying them together. A split second later Turpin collided with the other side of the door, his irate face glaring at her through the glass. "Just give us the scale, Hayley, and we'll leave you alone!"

"Yeah, right!" she yelled back.

Turpin's face disappeared and was replaced by Fulcher's fist, which smashed clear through the glass and started to untie Hayley's hoodie from the handles. Hayley spun around and scrambled up the steps, tripping for a moment and bashing her knee hard. No time to think about the pain now; she had to move.

Hayley burst out into the fresh air of the rooftop and slid the heavy bolt across the steel door behind her. That should keep even that monster of a woman busy for a little while. There was no other way down from the roof, but she had a plan. She limped over to the old plant bed, plunged her hand into the mucky soil, and pulled out the scale. She stowed it in her backpack and took a breath. Now all she needed to do was call the police again (zero points for originality, but, hey, it worked last time), then she could sit back and wait for the goons chasing her to retreat once more. She reached into her pocket for her phone. It wasn't there. She tried her other pockets, checked her backpack—nothing.

Knock, knock. The steel door.

"If you're looking for your phone, Miss Hicks, simply open the door and I will be happy to return it to you."

Oh no. It must have fallen out of her pocket when she tripped on the stairs.

The door rattled as Fulcher commenced her assault from the other side. The hinges groaned under the attack. It wouldn't take her long to get through.

That's that, then, thought Hayley. She was going to be captured. They were going to get the scale and . . . then what? They didn't seem like the sort of people who left witnesses behind. It would be very easy for them to make it look like she'd "accidentally" fallen off the roof.

But as she kept her eyes fixed on the shaking door, Hayley was shocked to feel a sharp tap on her shoulder. Without thinking, she spun into an improvised roundhouse kick—but when it connected with her attacker with a dull *clang,* she felt like she'd kicked a wall. She hopped up and down, rubbing her throbbing foot. "OWW!"

"Sorry! Are you all right?"

The apology was coming from the knight in gleaming white armor standing before her on the rooftop.

The Defender.

It was official. There was nothing left that would surprise her today. Hayley stopped rubbing her foot and scanned around for something to protect herself with, in case this weirdo tried anything funny. Although, now that she looked at him properly, he didn't seem like he was about to attack her. In fact, if it hadn't been for the strange, sleek armor and the sword hanging by his waist, she would have said his body language looked kind of . . . nervous.

"I didn't mean to surprise you," muttered the Defender, his voice obscured by his helmet.

Hayley was puzzled. This wasn't the same brave superhero she'd seen at the Tower. He reminded her of some of the boys at her school, who had no idea how to talk to girls.

"No worries," said Hayley. "Sorry I kicked you."

For his part, Alfie hadn't had time to think about what he was going to say if he found Hayley Hicks. How were superheroes supposed to talk anyway? He hadn't felt much like one five minutes ago, screaming and clinging on to Wyvern's spectral mane as they galloped across the sky. He'd only opened his eyes when Wyvern started her dive down toward the tower-block roof—and even then he'd regretted it. The landing zone looked like a postage stamp from the air. He was glad no one had been there to witness him fall flat on his face as Wyvern disappeared back into his spurs an inch from the roof. Hayley had emerged a few moments later, hardly giving him enough time to find his feet and hide behind the water tank. He'd watched as she retrieved the scale from the plant bed and then, when he heard the people who were chasing her, he thought he should make his move.

Hayley stepped closer, staring at Alfie's impenetrable visor. "You seem smaller than I remember," she said.

Alfie shifted uncomfortably. This wasn't territory he wanted to get into, but Hayley was poking the chest plate of the armor, fascinated. " 'May you never die a yeoman warder.' That's what you said to that poor beefeater. What does it mean?"

"I did?" Alfie was confused. He stepped backward, stumbled over an air duct, and fell on his back with a clatter.

Alfie heaved himself onto his feet while Hayley watched, unimpressed. "I thought you were supposed to be, like, this big hero or something."

Alfie laughed. "You and me both."

The steel door started to bend as Fulcher put her whole weight against it from the other side. Alfie decided he'd better get to the point. "The lizard scale. I need it."

Hayley tightened her grip on her backpack. "Why?"

"It's complicated . . . there's no time to . . ." Alfie stood up straight and did his best to look intimidating. "I could just take it off you," he said.

"I suppose so. But something tells me you won't," said Hayley as she shot a glance to the shaking door. "I'll make you a deal. I'll give you what you want. But first, you have to get me out of here. I know you have a ride."

"What? No! I can't. That's not allowed. It's against the—"

BANG!

The door to the roof flew off its hinges, and Turpin and Fulcher barreled out behind it. If they were startled to see the Defender there, they were too professional to show it.

"HEY! SIR THINKS-A-LOT! LET'S GO!" Hayley screamed at Alfie, whacking him across his shoulder plate.

Before he was even conscious of commanding Wyvern to appear, the ghost horse leapt out of his spurs and Alfie hauled Hayley up behind him. Fulcher lunged at them, her hand passing through Wyvern's wispy legs as they dived off the roof.

"HOLD ON!" said Alfie.

Hayley's stomach lurched as they plummeted toward the ground and buzzed low over a playground. Once past, they climbed steeply again, missing trees and telephone wires by inches. Alfie grappled with the reins, trying to at least make it look like he was directing the horse, but Hayley wasn't fooled.

"DO YOU EVEN KNOW HOW TO RIDE THIS THING?!" she yelled over the rushing wind.

The thumping noise of rotor blades filled the air as a sleek, black helicopter descended into their path.

"LOOK OUT!" Hayley shouted.

But Wyvern had spotted the danger. She slalomed around the helicopter and powered between two tall buildings, close enough to see the shocked faces of the residents at the windows. Alfie risked a glance back. The chopper rose above the buildings and pointed its nose after them. They weren't out of the woods yet—not even close.

"GIVE ME THE SCALE AND I'LL FIND SOMEWHERE TO DROP YOU OFF!" Alfie shouted.

Hayley looked down at the streets below—they were crawling with the flashing blue lights of police cars. "NO WAY! YOU'RE NOT GETTING ANYTHING TILL I'M SAFE!"

Alfie didn't know what to do. LC had said he must retrieve the lizard's scale at all costs. But this girl was an innocent in all this; he couldn't just leave her to the mercy of whoever was chasing them.

Suddenly a second black helicopter swept into sight on their left, joining the pursuit. Wyvern banked away. Hayley screamed and pointed to their right—a third helicopter drifted into view, even closer than the other two. Wyvern zigzagged wildly, trying to shake off their pursuers.

"WYVERN, TAKE US HOME!" commanded Alfie.

The horse whinnied and bucked—she obviously didn't think much of that idea.

"JUST DO IT!"

The horse seemed to gather herself for a moment before powering high into the sky at a furious gallop, heading for the clouds.

SEVENTEEN

The Lost Crown

Wind kicked up a sandstorm from the floor as Wyvern descended back into the Arena, the roof spiraling shut behind her.

The Lord Chamberlain hurried over, shielding his eyes. "Did you get the lizard's scale? Sir?"

Inside his armor, Alfie bit his lip and wondered how to begin. This was going to be messy. "Yep. And that's not all I brought back. Now don't over-react, LC, but . . ."

Hayley leaned out from behind Alfie. She smiled and waved. "Hiya."

The Lord Chamberlain rocked backward like he'd been punched. Brian was just walking back in, eating a sandwich. Bread and cheese fell to the ground as he dived to the nearest wall and pulled on a long red rope. Alarm bells pealed.

Wyvern retreated inside her spurs, depositing Alfie and Hayley onto their feet, their legs still wobbly from the ride. Yeoman warders brandishing pikes surrounded Hayley, and as Alfie held his hands up in a vain attempt to calm everyone down,

Brian bundled him behind a nearby column. On a balcony overlooking the Arena, a Gatling gun mounted on iron wheels rolled forward, manned by a fearsome-looking female beefeater.

Hayley put her hands up. "Everyone, chill. This wasn't my idea."

"She's right. It was mine." Alfie shrugged off Brian and reached up to remove his armor.

"DON'T!" blurted LC.

But it was too late. Alfie's magical armor disappeared in a flash. He stood in front of Hayley in his T-shirt and boxers and shrugged. Hayley opened her mouth to say something, but no words came out, just a high-pitched squeak.

Alfie pulled on some clothes, while the Lord Chamberlain paced up and down, turning an interesting shade of purple.

"Do you realize what you've done, sir? I told you, it is the number one rule. You do *not* reveal your identity to *anyone*, let alone some . . . some . . . girl. You were only with her for five minutes! What happened?"

"There were agents! And helicopters! Three of them! We had to get out of there. What was I supposed to do, drop her in the Thames?"

LC's expression suggested he wouldn't have been against the idea.

Meanwhile, Brian stared at the bewildered

Hayley, his arms folded. He wasn't going to take his eyes off this intruder. A friendly lady yeoman handed Hayley a glass of water and offered her a chair. Brian scowled, but the kind beefeater stuck her tongue out at him and sauntered off.

"So I'm guessing this place doesn't appear in any of the guidebooks?" said Hayley, trying and failing to raise a smile from Brian.

LC rubbed his weary face, then waved his hand at Hayley, defeated. "She stays here. For now."

"WHAT? But she's an outsider!" said Brian.

"I am aware of that! However, we cannot become sidetracked; there is too much work to be done. Under no circumstances is she to leave the Tower."

"Hello? I have rights too, you know," said Hayley. "Don't I get to see a lawyer or something?"

But the others ignored her protests. Alfie tried in vain to referee the argument, as LC maintained that Hayley was "only" a girl. The best thing to do was keep a close eye on her until the crisis had passed, rather than have her running around outside telling everyone heaven knows what; Brian yelled that there were plenty of empty dungeons deep in the Tower, reserved for "little problems" just like this one. In the end Hayley gave up trying to get their attention and took to gazing around the astonishing underground hall instead. She'd never seen anything like it, even on all those day trips to castles and historical houses with her gran.

Hayley's eyes were drawn to a small crop of flickering candles surrounding a framed picture of a familiar-looking beefeater. Standing up slowly, she crossed to the shrine, followed by the beefeater guards. Sure enough, the man in the photo was the same beefeater she had watched draw his last breath in the fight at the Tower. It was a face she would never forget. It was nice to see him in happier times, his eyes alive with pride and inner steel. "What was his name?" she asked.

Alfie, LC, and Brian stopped arguing and looked over to her.

"Rosie," said Brian. "It was his nickname. Warrant Officer William Flowers. Rosie. You see?"

Hayley picked up a long white candle from a packet next to the shrine, lit it, and placed it gently alongside the others. When she turned around again, there were tears in her eyes. "The truth is, I haven't got anywhere else to go. Nowhere I want to be, anyway. I can't pretend that I've got a clue what's going on here, but from what I've seen, you're the good guys."

She reached into her backpack. The beefeaters readied their pikes. "If I can help you stop that . . . *thing*, then count me in."

Hayley opened her hand to reveal the Black Lizard's scale.

• • •

Alfie and Hayley sat on one of the long benches that lined the side of the Arena, watching Brian don a protective visor, light a blowtorch, and direct it at the Black Lizard's scale, which was secured in a vise.

"My gran would go nuts for all this. She loves you royals," said Hayley.

Alfie smiled. "That's nice."

"I think you're a bunch of spoiled, sponging parasites."

Alfie winced. "Fair enough. A lot of people think that."

Sparks flew off the surface of the scale, but when Brian pulled the flame away, there wasn't so much as a mark left on it. He frowned, tossed the blowtorch away, and picked up a sledgehammer.

"It's nothing personal, yeah?" Hayley drained her tea. "It's just, I mean, who died and made you king?"

"My dad," said Alfie.

Hayley looked shocked, then burst out laughing. Alfie dissolved into laughter too. The Lord Chamberlain shuffled uneasily, unsure how to handle this outbreak of giggling.

Brian's sledgehammer snapped in two. "STUPID THING!" he yelled, throwing it down and picking up a chain saw.

"So that wasn't you I saw fighting the lizard the other night?" asked Hayley. "It was your dad? Figures."

"Yeah," said Alfie. "Wait, what's that supposed to mean?"

A shower of sparks erupted from the scale as Brian brought the teeth of the chain saw down on it. Suddenly the black scale shot free of the vise, flew through the air, skimmed over Alfie's and Hayley's heads, and embedded itself in the wall behind them.

Brian wiped his brow and shrugged. "Want my expert opinion? Beats me."

"Mind if I have a go?" asked Alfie.

He strode across the Arena, opened the velvet curtains, and parted the tapestry to reveal the Regalia Cabinet.

"MAJESTY, NO!" exclaimed LC, too late.

Hayley gawked in amazement at the sparkling Crown Jewels.

"Just pretend you haven't seen any of that, if you wouldn't mind, miss," LC sighed.

"Wait a minute, so those ones upstairs *are* fakes? Gran was right!" said Hayley.

"Gran? Who is Gran?" LC was getting in a flap.

"Relax, LC," said Alfie as he picked out the Sword of State from the cabinet.

The others covered their eyes as the sword burst into life in response to its master's touch.

"Wow!" said Hayley, getting up from the bench.

Brian pulled the black scale out of the wall and dropped it at Alfie's feet. "When you've quite finished showing off to your lady friend . . . ," he said.

Alfie aimed the tip of the sword over the scale and plunged it down, slicing it clean in two.

Brian picked up the fragments, clearly impressed. "So the question is, where does the Black Lizard get a hide so tough that nothing except the Defender's sword can scratch it?"

Alfie looked to LC. The old man's lips were moving ever so slightly, but nothing was coming out. His skin was turning ashen before their eyes. "LC, are you OK?"

Hayley and Alfie took an arm each and eased him onto a bench. He was mumbling, his eyes distant, lost in a world of his own.

"Why didn't I see this before? The White Horse. He found it at the White Horse. I've been such a fool."

Brian gave the kids a worried look, then booted LC lightly in the shin.

"Ow!"

"Sorry, boss, but you lost it for a minute there. What's up?"

The Lord Chamberlain sprang to his feet and dashed for the door. "The Archives! We must look in the Archives!"

Back in the Map Room, a pair of beefeaters rolled back an enormous, dusty rug to reveal a hidden hatch the size of a barn door. Alfie and Hayley lent Brian a hand as he heaved it open. Beneath the hatch, three old wooden ladders coated with cobwebs stretched down into darkness. Stale air rose to greet them.

"Now, does anyone have a dust allergy?" LC was buzzing with nervous energy.

Alfie and Hayley looked into the bottomless pit and exchanged a glance.

"Yeah, because that would be the only reason not to go down there," said Hayley.

But apparently they had no choice in the matter—LC would need them to carry "the scrolls."

The ladder felt anything but secure beneath Alfie's feet. The wood was brittle, and there was a gap every yard or so where a rung had completely rotted away. Brian had insisted on climbing underneath Alfie, in case he needed catching. Hayley, on the next ladder, tried not to take his lack of chivalry personally. LC, on the third ladder, called up to the beefeaters to give them some light.

Gas lamps on ropes were lowered past them into the abyss. As the enormous circular cavern around them was illuminated, Alfie and Hayley gazed in awe at row upon row of thick wooden shelves, drawers, and odd compartments. Each one was stuffed to overflowing with parchments, ancient leather-bound tomes, and rolled-up canvases.

"I hope you remembered your library card," muttered Brian, clearly unimpressed with their subterranean excursion.

"What is all this stuff?" asked Alfie.

"This *stuff*, as you put it," replied LC, "is the history of the United Kingdom. The *real* history."

"You have heard of these new things they've got called COM-PU-TERS, haven't you?" said Hayley as she picked a cobweb as thick as a scarf off her shoulder.

LC pushed off from a shelf, propelling his ladder sideways around the rim of the Archive. "This way!"

The others realized he was expecting them to follow and very slowly edged their way around toward him. The old man was already pulling out dusty manuscripts and scrolls and passing them along, until each of them had as much as they could carry in one hand.

"Now don't drop any, or you'll have to go down and fetch them. And, believe me, if you think the climb down was hard, the climb up is a great deal worse!"

And with that, LC began ascending once more. Gripping as hard as they could without crumpling the tomes they were holding, the others clawed their way back up the ladders, until finally they collapsed into the Map Room, tipping their heavy loads onto the floor. The Lord Chamberlain was already on his hands and knees, unfurling parchments, scanning the lines of tightly bunched, ornate writing in a strange language the others didn't recognize.

"I told you that Alfred the Great was granted powers by his ancestor gods, yes? But I never told you the whole legend—"

"Wait a second—rewind," Hayley said. "Gods?"

Frustrated, LC tossed more and more of the ancient scrolls aside. The others dodged as page after page skittered past their feet.

"Yes, yes, the ancient gods. Honestly, I never thought the details were all that accurate. The older the myth, the more it tends to have been varnished over the centuries. But now I fear . . . Oh, where is it?"

LC was left with just one scroll. He unraveled it carefully and held it up to the light. "Aha!" He laid it down in front of them. Amid the curious scrawled writing there was a drawing of King Alfred the Great, kneeling among a familiar circle of tall stones, holding aloft a newly forged, golden crown.

"That's Stonehenge," said Alfie.

"Indeed, Majesty," replied LC. "According to some sources, that is where Alfred went to pray to his ancestors for help. The crown was said to have been a gift from the ancient gods. The source of his power."

"So where is it now?" asked Hayley. "You still got it in your little treasure chest back there?"

LC frowned—he wasn't even close to being comfortable having this outsider around yet. "No, Miss Hicks. The chronicles claim that King Alfred, fearful of the awesome power the crown could bestow should it fall into the wrong hands, broke it into four parts and had it scattered far and wide, hidden at secret sites across his kingdom. Even so, by then the Defender's power had been absorbed into the king's blood and was passed to his descendants upon the Succession. I had always assumed Alfred's crown was merely symbolic—a metaphor—but if it is real . . ."

Alfie was beginning to understand the reason LC was so concerned. "You think the Black Lizard is trying to find the pieces of Alfred's crown? To do what? Reassemble it?"

"Yes . . . and I fear he may be halfway there already."

LC hurried across the hall to the ops table. Taking his first closer look at the giant map, Alfie noticed an array of strange markings—not the normal county lines he was used to seeing on modern maps of the country, but rather the boundaries of the ancient kingdoms of Northumbria, Mercia, and Wessex. Instead of motorways, ancient ley lines crisscrossed the landscape. Peculiar symbols were marked here and there—a heraldic shield, a coiled serpent, a unicorn.

LC grabbed one of the Black Lizard figurines and used a rake to push it toward a picture of a white horse in the southwest corner of the map.

"Three months ago we received reports of an unauthorized dig here, at the Westbury White Horse. You know it?"

Alfie and Hayley shook their heads, and LC flapped his hands impatiently.

"Of course you do. A big horse carved in chalk into the hillside in the West Country? Well, there were tons of earth displaced at night. We thought it was just pointless vandalism. But legend has it that the horse carved into that hill marks the site of Edington—Alfred the Great's final victory against the Vikings. If Alfred were to choose somewhere to bury a part of his crown, that would be as good a spot as any."

"And you think our scaly friend found a piece there?" asked Alfie.

"Yes. And then he went looking for more. The Tower was an obvious place to try—it houses the Crown Jewels, after all. But he had more luck at Stonehenge."

He pushed a second Black Lizard figurine over to the image of the standing stones in the west.

"I believe he found a second piece there—that's why he was so much stronger—strong enough to kill your father."

Hayley gave Alfie a sympathetic glance.

"The remaining two pieces may have been moved over the years," LC continued. "In medieval times many treasure troves were dumped into the Thames to be retrieved later. The Black Lizard must have had good reason to search there, but he came away empty-handed."

"Well, that's good news," said Alfie hopefully.

Brian whistled through his teeth. "That fella's tough enough with half the crown; I'd hate to think what he'd be like if he gets the whole set."

The Lord Chamberlain's face darkened. "If the Black Lizard reforges the whole of Alfred's crown, then he will wield immense power."

Alfie was starting to understand. "More than the Defender . . ."

LC nodded. "Such a creature would be more than a king. He could be a great and terrible emperor. Democracy swept aside. Every man, woman, and child in the country enslaved. An absolute monarch, unstoppable, even by the Defender. I fear the kingdom would be plunged into a second Dark Age."

The beefeaters had stopped their work. Alfie felt their eyes on him, looking for some indication that he could turn the tide, some sign of hope. It was Hayley who broke the silence, punching Alfie on the shoulder.

"Come on, then, hero boy. What are you going to do about it?"

-EIGHTEEN-

Around Britain by Flying Horse

Wyvern didn't like him. Alfie knew that and he was cool with it. He didn't need the respect of a see-through flying horse to feel good about himself. He could put up with the moody snorting, the irritable mane-shaking, even the outright petulant bucking of the back legs every time he asked her to do something. But actually trying to kill him? That's where he drew the line. Because, in the end, a superhero's sidekick has to know who's boss.

They were in a steady cruise about ten thousand feet up when it happened. Wyvern was galloping beneath a bladelike moon, carrying the Defender on his mission to search for the remaining fragments of Alfred the Great's crown. Far below, the fields and villages of Somerset sped past. Alfie was enjoying himself. OK, that was a lie. Alfie still squeezed his eyes shut in terror whenever Wyvern powered through the banks of clouds that rose up in front of them. It looked like you were speeding headfirst into a brick wall, and it was such a surprise to come out the other side without feeling a thing. But he was at least starting to feel more confident.

"You should be there soon, Your Majesty." The Lord Chamberlain's voice was tinny, but distinct, in Alfie's new radio earpiece.

"You're looking for King Alfred's Monument; it's a relatively modern memorial stone on the Isle of Athelney. Your namesake built an abbey on that spot to commemorate one of his victories over the Vikings a thousand years ago. He might have buried part of his original crown there."

While LC and Brian had been deciding on a target list of sites for Alfie to search, Hayley had made herself useful, rigging up a communication system for the Defender's armor. She couldn't believe how primitive the Tower HQ was technology-wise, and kept saying how her gran's old flat was better equipped.

"You're telling me this is magic armor, but there's no way you can even talk to each other when Alfie is out and about?" she'd demanded of a bemused Lord Chamberlain. "That's kind of lame."

The Lord Chamberlain had stared at Hayley like she was a time traveler from the distant future who had just crash-landed into his world. "We updated everything very recently, I'll have you know," he had spluttered.

"Oh yeah, when?"

"1948!"

After that, Brian had rustled up a modern radio from the guardroom, and soon Hayley was going to work. Alfie had watched her, fingers a blur, as she strip-mined the radio for parts. Given more time and resources, Hayley had said she could whip up a whole communication rig with portable cameras too.

"Er . . . roger that, control," replied Alfie, copying the radio chatter he'd once heard in an old war movie.

Wyvern flew on, breaking through the clouds and offering Alfie a glimpse of the stars above them.

LC sounded unsure in his ear. "Um . . . good? Roger back. Hayley, are you sure this wretched thing is on?" Alfie could picture LC back at the Keep, hunched over the radio transmitter like it might explode in his hands. "Now be careful out there, sir, we can't afford for you to—"

Alfie didn't hear the rest, because that was when Wyvern suddenly screamed as if in unbearable pain and disappeared from beneath him back into his spurs.

"WYVERN! NO! COME BACK!" Alfie yelled as he plummeted.

"SPURS! SPURS! SPUUUURS!"

But the stubborn horse wouldn't emerge. Panicked, Alfie looked around at the sky as he spun around. Was the Black Lizard here? Was that why Wyvern had freaked out? But the sky was dark and empty. Upside down, in a flat spin, the ground approaching fast, Alfie pawed at his armor, searching for a rip cord.

"PARACHUTE?!" Alfie shouted in desperation, but nothing happened.

Trees, hedges, a silent country road, all were coming up to meet him fast. *I'm going to be the first Defender to die falling off his own horse.*

With twenty feet to spare, Wyvern burst from the spurs and Alfie grabbed the reins. His only thought was to find a soft landing, which they did, seconds later. Well, soft*ish*. Boy and horse snapped their way through the branches of a small wood before finally shuddering to a stop next to an ancient oak tree.

Alfie slumped on Wyvern's back, checking that nothing was broken. The smell of wet leaves and soil filled his nostrils. The armor had saved him from harm—he wasn't even scratched. Not that he could say the same for the trees in the woods;

they'd carved a corridor of destruction right through them. Angry, Alfie grabbed his horse's great neck and pulled up her head until they were eye to eye.

"What was that all about? You could have killed me!"

The horse reared up, screaming in pain again.

"What?! What did I do?"

The horse stamped the ground and spun around, uncontrollable. Her hooves kicked the trunk of the great oak, shaking it to its roots and bringing down a rain of twigs and leaves.

"WYVERN, CUT IT OUT!"

But shouting seemed to make the bucking and rearing worse. He needed to calm down, get a grip. *I'm trying to reason with a magical horse*, Alfie thought as he held on to the reins, making the horse walk in a calming circle.

Eventually the creature settled, giving Alfie a chance to get his bearings. The moonlight revealed a great, grassy plain beyond the woods. There was a sleeping farmhouse perhaps half a mile away, and still farther, a pile of cracked and broken rocks. With a gasp, Alfie realized what was wrong with Wyvern. He kept his voice low and soothing.

"It's Stonehenge, isn't it, girl?" They must have flown right over it—*that's* why she'd gone so crazy. "You remember what happened there, don't you?"

Wyvern reared up. Alfie fought to control her, yanking down on the reins.

"HEY! Stop it! I miss him too, all right? Just give me a break, would you? I'm doing the best I can with all this new . . . *stuff.*"

Alfie slapped his chest plate, the thud echoing around the woods. "So calm down and start acting like the king's horse, or I'm putting you back in your spurs, permanently."

Alfie rattled his spurs provocatively. But how else could he get home if not with Wyvern? Maybe he could take the tunic off, make the armor disappear, and hitchhike? No, he'd be recognized in a second. Alfie remembered the earpiece and microphone he was wearing, but he couldn't get through to anyone back at the Keep. The radio must have been broken in the crash. *They'll be worried sick,* he thought.

Alfie realized that Wyvern had stopped her pacing beneath him and was standing patient and calm, like she was waiting for orders. Surprised, he stroked her ears and flanks and she whinnied gently. Alfie couldn't explain it, but he felt more connected to Wyvern. He barely had to squeeze his legs to make her turn this way and that at his command. She was suddenly *his* horse. Maybe his little outburst had worked. Alfie smiled to himself and patted her again. A small victory.

"Good girl. How about we go and find the rest of Alfred's crown before that big lizard does?"

Wyvern stamped her front hooves in approval. In the blink of an eye they were shooting back into the sky.

. . .

Every night for the next week, Alfie and Wyvern searched the length and breadth of England and Wales for the remaining pieces of Alfred's crown. But they found nothing. The Isle of Athelney turned out to be a grassy hill with a simple stone marker showing where an ancient abbey had once stood. In Alfred the Great's time, it had been sur-rounded by marshes, but now it was just fields. Alfie had unhooked his Scout Orb from his belt and held it in the palm of his hand, before com-manding it to "seek." To his amazement, the Orb glowed, leapt into the air, and then burrowed down into the soil of the hill and disappeared. Alfie closed his eyes, just as Brian had instructed him to do. Suddenly he could see what the Orb could see, playing out in front of him like he was looking at a television screen in the darkness: stones, rubble, tree roots, but no sign of any fragments of Alfred's crown. LC had said it would "glow like a hot coal" and be easy to see, but there was nothing here except cold, dark soil.

St. Bartholomew's Parish Church in Winchester was the next stop, on the site where King Alfred had been buried. His bones had long been lost, but LC had reasoned that a piece of his crown might have been buried with him and could perhaps still be there in the foundations. Alfie and Wyvern had landed unseen on the roof of the church, while the people below passed by, oblivious. Alfie dispatched the Scout Orb to sweep through the dark, empty building, but there was no hint of any crown fragments there either.

It was the same story the following night at Alfred the Great's birthplace, the small town of Wantage, in Oxfordshire. A grand statue of the king still stood in the marketplace, though one of his arms (the one holding an ax) had been snapped off by bored local youths. Alfie was exhausted— days of official duties followed by nights flying around the countryside as the Defender had not left much time for sleep. So while the Scout Orb burrowed beneath the statue, he sat down at its base for a rest. There he found an inscription:

ALFRED FOUND LEARNING DEAD,
AND HE RESTORED IT.
EDUCATION NEGLECTED
AND HE REVIVED IT.
THE LAWS POWERLESS

AND HE GAVE THEM FORCE.
THE CHURCH DEBASED
AND HE RAISED IT.
THE LAND RAVAGED BY A FEARFUL ENEMY,
FROM WHICH HE DELIVERED IT.
ALFRED'S NAME SHALL LIVE AS LONG
AS MANKIND SHALL RESPECT THE PAST.

"No pressure, then," Alfie muttered to himself.
"*VICTORY!*"

The shout echoed across the hillside as Alfie felt himself pull his sword from the animal's side. He was back on the battlefield of Edington, gazing down at a pile of slain devil dogs—had he done that? Suddenly the ground shook beneath his feet. Breaking through the trees of a nearby copse came a Viking ten times larger than any that lay dead around him. A true giant, with monstrous features, raging like a wild beast. Somehow he knew his name. It was Guthrum, the Viking Lord. They charged at each other across the field, and when they met, their swords clashed with an explosion of light that lit up the sky for miles around.

Alfie gasped as he came around from the vision. He shook his head and looked up to spot a police constable strolling through the marketplace on his late-night patrol. Alfie just had time to hide behind his ancestor's statue as the policeman walked past.

. . .

On the seventh night of fruitless searching, Alfie trudged back into the Keep and removed the tunic, happy to feel the armor disappear from his limbs. He collapsed into an old leather sofa, and Herne jumped up with him, resting his shaggy head in his lap. Alfie yawned . . . and Herne copied him.

Hayley breezed in carrying a box of take-out pizza. "Get it while it's hot!"

Happy to forget about the mission for a while, Alfie leapt up and grabbed a piece, chewing fast. Then he frowned. Something was wrong. "There's no pepperoni on this."

"Veggie." Hayley shrugged. "It's healthier anyway. You're supposed to be a superhero; you should at least eat right." She smiled at Herne as he stretched out on the sofa. "It's been nice having him around—keeps me company when you're out and about, don't you, boy?" She leaned down to stroke him, but the dog let out a low growl, and she whipped her hand away. "Although we're not quite on stroking terms yet."

The Lord Chamberlain bustled in and went straight to the ops table, fussing over the markers that covered the map, showing all the places they had already searched. "I take it you drew another blank, sir?"

"Not a sausage. A bit like this pizza," said Alfie. "Are you sure that was a good lead?"

LC didn't reply, only frowned with concern. Alfie sighed inwardly. In many ways he was feeling pretty good about being the Defender. He was finally friends with Wyvern, he was learning how to use most of the Regalia, and now that he had Hayley to talk to when he got back at night, he didn't feel so bad about keeping the truth from his brother and sister. He didn't want LC bringing him down.

"Hey, at least there's still no Black Lizard around, right?" Alfie said hopefully.

The old man gazed down at the map, lost in thought. "That's what concerns me, Majesty. That beast has been one step ahead of us the whole way. I fear it's only a matter of time before he makes a strike for another crown fragment. But where? We've searched in every conceivable place—"

The old man stopped and pointed at the pizza like it was a murder weapon in a courtroom.

"Wait a moment . . . where did you get *that*?"

Hayley shrugged. "The . . . pizzeria. You know, I ordered it on the phone and a little man on a moped came and delivered it."

"To the *Keep*? To our secret base that has lain undiscovered for centuries? Brian! Brian?!"

Hayley sighed. She'd been there for a week, but she was already used to LC's little blowups. "Count to ten or something, seriously. One of your beefy blokes in a skirt took it in upstairs. Your secret is safe."

LC turned bright red with anger. "They're called yeoman warders. If you're going to stay here, young lady, then at least do us the courtesy of learning the correct terminology!"

"Whatever." Hayley picked up another slice of pizza and shoved it in her mouth.

Alfie could feel the last of his good mood slipping away. He could see that the stress was getting to everyone. Hayley hadn't even been out of the Tower since she'd arrived. She was probably going a little stir-crazy. He leaned over and whispered to her. "Hey, Hayley. Why don't we take a ride?"

NINETEEN

How the Other Half Lives

Hayley was looking, unconvinced, at the old carriage sitting at the mouth of the tunnel in the secret antechamber. "I thought I wasn't allowed out?"

"I won't tell if you don't," said Alfie. "Besides, you need a change of scene."

Hayley smiled. It was true. She'd lived through the weirdest and most exciting week of her life all in one place. She'd even been sleeping on the old leather sofa next to the ops table, with only one of Herne's old blankets to keep her warm. The chief yeoman warder had brought her a pay-as-you-go cell phone so she could at least call her gran and check that she was OK. Hayley was desperate to go and see her, but at least she sounded cheerful and said she liked the "hotel" she thought she was staying in.

"I don't usually go out with strangers," said Hayley.

"How can you call me a stranger? You know more about me than almost anyone."

Alfie jumped on board and held the door open. "Hop on. I want to show you my place."

Hayley stepped into the carriage. "Very Cinderella," she smirked.

"Now hang on tight. This thing is faster than it looks," said Alfie. He pulled down her safety bar.

And with that, they rolled forward, getting faster and faster until the tunnel around them was a blur of speed.

In the end, Hayley insisted that they make the trip from the Tower to the palace twice, the second time so she could keep her eyes open and not scream so much. She'd always loved a good shot of adrenaline. Riding in the supercharged carriage was like gulping down a dozen energy drinks all at once; her heart was thumping and her eyes were wide with excitement. Alfie did his best to pretend he enjoyed the rush as much as she did.

By the time they'd climbed the secret spiral staircase into Alfie's bedroom, it was past one o'clock in the morning. But Alfie gave Hayley the grand tour anyway, occasionally ducking out of the way of a servant on a late-night errand. Through ballrooms, libraries, and drawing rooms, Hayley marveled at the grand oil paintings and ornate wallpaper flecked with gold. She gaped at piles of antique furniture. "How the other half lives, eh?"

The Tower had been impressive in an ancient-castle kind of way, but Buckingham Palace was in another league. Hayley couldn't believe Alfie could even call it *home*; the word was just too small for this place.

In the long Picture Gallery, Alfie showed her the portraits of long-dead kings and queens. "Don't you ever get freaked out with all these eyes watching you the whole time?"

Alfie shrugged. "You get used to it. Dad liked to come here sometimes. I always wondered why, but now I get it. It's like you don't want to let them down or something."

"Team Defender, huh?" Hayley looked at Alfie. He cut a lonely and slight figure with all his ancestors staring down at him. "I'm sure your dad would be proud of you."

Alfie smiled. It was nice to hear, even if he doubted it was true. "What about *your* dad? Won't he be missing you?" He knew immediately it was the wrong thing to ask, as Hayley's smile dissolved.

"My dad never wanted to know me. I don't even know where he lives."

Alfie's mind sparked into damage-control mode: "Do you want some ice cream? Oh, wait. Do you eat that kind of thing?"

"I'm a veggie, Alfie, not a monk," she snapped,

then took a deep breath and tried again. "That sounds nice, thanks."

The palace kitchens were empty at this time of night. Hayley whistled, impressed, as the strip lighting illuminated a hundred feet of stainless steel counters and cookers. Alfie opened up a freezer and rummaged around inside, retrieving a selection of the largest ice cream tubs Hayley had ever seen. They ate chocolate chip, caramel toffee, pistachio, blueberry, and something that was either watermelon or mango (they couldn't decide). Hayley had never eaten so much in one go before.

"I'm sorry I dragged you into all this," Alfie said.

She shrugged. "Beats going into some foster home. Mind you, I could do with my own room again. LC isn't exactly a fun roommate."

"We'd better get back before he realizes you've gone AWOL."

"Yeah. He doesn't need to worry, though. I wouldn't tell anyone about all this. I mean . . . who'd believe me anyway?"

• • •

Back in Alfie's bedroom, they were still laughing about precisely how much LC and Brian would both flip out if they knew what they'd been doing, when there was a knock at the door. They stared at each other, alarmed, then Alfie quickly opened the entrance to the secret staircase and gestured for Hayley to go through.

Knock-knock-knock.

"Hang on!" he called out.

Hayley was safely on the staircase, but in his haste to close the door, Alfie knocked the contents of the dressing table onto the floor. A can of deodorant had gotten itself wedged in the mechanism, stopping the secret entrance from closing up.

Another sharp series of knocks. The bedroom door started to open. "Alfie?"

Alfie dived to the door, stopping it from opening too far.

It was Richard, dressed in a Harrow School T-shirt and pajama bottoms. "You rearranging your furniture or what?"

Behind Alfie, Hayley reached back into the room and yanked at the deodorant can, trying to move it. Alfie winced and coughed to cover the noise. "I didn't know you were here tonight, Rich?"

"Rugby match against Westminster. Thought I'd swing by, stay the night." Richard was straining to see over Alfie's shoulder. "I heard laughing."

"You know me. I'm an idiot. Ha, ha, all the time. Sometimes for no reason." It was just as well that the lights were off, because he could feel himself blushing.

"A *girl* laughing." Richard cocked an eyebrow. "Where were you tonight, anyway?"

Alfie knew if he could just keep Richard talking, Hayley would be able to get the secret door closed. "Oh, you know, more coronation prep. Boredom central. LC is going crazy with all the rehearsals and stuff—"

Richard's question was just a bluff—he lowered his shoulder and shoved Alfie back into his room.

"No!" Alfie yelled as he spun around.

Richard flicked the lights on. But the room was empty, the dressing table back where it should be. "OK, sorry. No girls. Should have known. But I used to be able to tell when you were lying . . ."

Alfie smiled and tried to look relaxed. "Guess you're losing your touch. Now if you don't mind? His Majesty orders you to vacate the royal chambers." He faked a yawn.

"Don't let it go to your head. Anyway, you haven't been officially crowned yet. Night!" Richard flicked off the light switch and shut the door, leaving Alfie in darkness.

• • •

A little while later, Alfie and Hayley were back at the Keep, giggling about their close call. They were so full of energy that sleep was out of the question.

"Care to share the joke, Majesty?" LC had materialized in the doorway.

"Just, er . . . discussing strategy." Hayley pretended to study the ops table as Brian emerged, checking the rounds in his sidearm before holstering it.

"You'd better leave that kind of thing to the experts," he said.

Hayley put her hands on her hips. "What? I've got a brain too, you know," she shot back. "And from where I'm standing, this lizard thingy is running rings around you lot."

"And where does Miss Hayley Hicks of Watford think we should search for the last fragments of King Alfred the Great's shattered crown? We're all ears," LC said, chuckling.

Alfie sighed. He didn't know whether he could stomach another argument at this time of night. But Hayley was studying the ops table map and the little model letter Xs, which marked all the places Alfie had searched and come up empty-handed.

"What have you got against Scotland, then?" she asked.

Sure enough, although there were crosses all over England and Wales, there wasn't a single one north of the border.

"You should perhaps leave the history to me," LC scoffed. "Alfred the Great never even went to Scotland." But as he said it, his smile faded.

"LC?" Alfie said. "What is it?"

The Lord Chamberlain was rubbing his temples, like he was massaging the idea out of his head.

"As far as the chronicles tell, King Alfred the Great never traveled there. But his favorite grandson, Athelstan, invaded Scotland when he was king, and no one knows why. There were no battles recorded."

"What kind of invasion doesn't have any fighting?" Alfie asked.

LC nodded, warming to the idea. "Quite. What if Alfred entrusted a piece of the crown to him to hide later in the far north?"

"That's pretty much what I was thinking too," said Hayley. "If you need any more pointers, I'll be in my office."

She tossed a model X to the grumpy-looking Brian, who scrambled to catch it, then sauntered over to the sofa and lay down with her hands behind her head.

TWENTY

The Fire Beneath the Castle

The Defender was flying blind. The storm front had been chasing them all the way from London, and now the rain was so heavy that he couldn't see more than a few feet ahead. Forked lightning flared above them. Alfie knew that planes could survive being struck—he hoped it was the same with his armor. At least Wyvern seemed to know where they were going. She pointed her sleek head into the wind and powered north.

At last the clouds thinned and dawn broke over the deep pink-and-green patchwork of moorland below. The Scottish Borders. He remembered flying over them as a child, in a helicopter on the way to another summer holiday at Balmoral. It was the one place the whole family seemed to love spending time together, even his father. Weeks spent walking through sweet-smelling pine trees, making campfires in the grounds, relaxing away from the glare of the TV cameras and crowds.

Richard liked to go hunting with his father, but Alfie was never that into it. He'd once told his dad it was "against his principles," but in truth it had more to do with the fact that he was a terrible shot and scared of guns. King Henry had been heartbroken on the day they'd had to sell the entire estate to a hotel chain. Alfie recalled hearing him shouting at the prime minister on the phone about it. "The Balmoral Luxury Spa? It's humiliating!"

"Do you read us, Iron Eagle?" Hayley laughed in his ear, shaking him from his thoughts. She'd enjoyed coming up with different code names for him—none of which LC thought were appropriate. But that didn't stop her. Alfie liked how she made jokes no matter how serious the situation—it was her way of dealing with it, he guessed.

"I read you, Beefeater." LC was sure to hate that too, and he could hear the smile in Hayley's voice.

"Nice view you've got from up there."

As promised, Hayley had attached a tiny camera on a headband for Alfie to wear under his armor. Brian was sure it wouldn't work, but somehow it did and Hayley couldn't contain her glee. "You guys should pay me to be here." The camera meant Alfie didn't feel so alone, now that everyone back at the Keep could see what he was seeing.

"Stand by, incoming intel." Brian's voice crashed

the conversation. "Seismic activity, central Edinburgh, six minutes ago."

"Seismic?" Alfie wasn't sure if he'd heard him right. "You mean like an *earthquake?*"

Was it a coincidence? Or had the Black Lizard gotten there first? Wyvern adjusted her course, folded her legs up tight, and dived toward the capital.

Edinburgh looked smaller than he'd expected, nestled between the blue waters of the Firth of Forth on one side and the hulking shadows of mighty hills on the other. A cacophony of car alarms and sirens rose to greet Alfie as he approached the city center. Wyvern buzzed across neat blocks of slate-gray buildings, toward the main artery, the aptly named Princes Street. It was early, but people were pouring out of their homes, confused and scared. The groan of another tremor rattled windows and dislodged tiles from the rooftops.

"It's coming from the castle, sir. Look sharp." LC sounded worried, and Alfie didn't blame him.

Edinburgh Castle sat on a giant crag overlooking the city. The Royal Mile, with its pubs and tourist shops, rose gently to meet it on one side. On the other there was nothing but the sheer rock face, leading hundreds of feet down to a park below. Alfie twitched Wyvern's reins and she responded, descending for a low approach on the south side—that way they could rise silently up the cliff until they reached the castle walls. No one would see them coming.

As they shot up the cliff face, another tremor shook the city. Alfie thought he saw a fresh crack appear along the rock, but they were going too fast for him to be sure. Wyvern spun left as a block of stone tumbled from the battlements, missing them by inches. Rising over the wall, they found a scene of devastation. The castle's museum building was ablaze. Fresh scorch marks crisscrossed the upper yard, as if someone had gone mad with a flame-thrower. Bags and cameras lay where they had been dropped. At the Portcullis entrance gate, soldiers from the Royal Regiment of Scotland, in their tartan kilts and feathered caps, were busy evacuating the last of the tourists. The distant wails of police sirens echoed around the city.

"Alfie, be careful—the Black Lizard could be there already." It was Hayley's voice in his earpiece.

Wyvern spun back into Alfie's spurs as he touched down and scanned the deserted square. The wooden doors to a very small, plain stone chapel had been smashed off their hinges.

"Yeah, you could be right about that," said Alfie.

St. Margaret's Chapel was the oldest building in the castle: a white-walled, simple space with room for only six pews and a small altar under an archway. Alfie couldn't imagine why the Black Lizard would want to come in here when there were dozens of impressive banquet halls and towers to choose from on all sides. But the creature had been here all right. The altar was shoved onto its side, scattering candles and flowers, and a gaping hole had been smashed in the stone floor.

Alfie unsheathed his sword. The golden glow from the blade lit the way as he edged toward the hole, senses on high alert. As he got closer, Alfie was surprised to feel heat washing over him. He whispered as loud as he dared into his mic, "Something's on fire down there."

"Your armor should protect you." It was Brian. "But I wouldn't stand around in it too long—don't want you getting baked."

"Yeah, thanks. Let's see what we're dealing with, shall we?"

Alfie unhooked the Scout Orb from his belt and dropped it into the hole. He closed his eyes, and suddenly he could see what the Orb could see. The hole had been ripped into the roof of a tunnel, which sloped away beneath him. The only light came from the far end—a flickering, warm glow. As the Orb reached the end of the tunnel, Alfie turned his head from side to side. The Orb followed its master's movements, swiveling to give him a better view of his surroundings.

"I think I may have just found some kind of portal to the underworld," Alfie whispered.

The tunnel opened out into an immense cavern, lit by an intense fire burning below at a fathomless depth. He heard something—a strange scratching. Alfie willed the Orb to look up and move closer, which it did, showing him another tunnel entrance on the other side of the great chasm. Through the heat haze he could see movement . . . the shadow of a person bent over something, digging. As he watched, the shadow twitched and convulsed, then, with a series of hideous cracks and groans, it transformed from a human into the unmistakable form of the hulking Black Lizard.

Flames shot outward, blinding Alfie. In the chapel above, he opened his eyes and gasped—it was almost as if he'd been standing in the fire himself. A moment later the Orb whistled out of the hole in the floor and returned to his hand. It was almost too hot to hold, even through his armored glove. Alfie wiped the film of soot off its surface and hooked the Orb back onto his belt.

"What did you see, sir?" asked LC.

"He's here. The lizard. But it was a man—the Black Lizard is a man."

"Has he found another piece of the crown?"

"Guess not, or he'd be gone by now." Alfie gripped the hilt of his sword. He could feel the power flowing through him and into the weapon. It didn't get rid of his nerves entirely, but it helped. "Let's see if I can get there first this time."

Alfie dropped into the tunnel. He had walked into a sauna once and turned around and walked right out again. He didn't get how anyone could find that sort of temperature fun. He'd barely been able to breathe, let alone relax. But that was nothing compared with the heat down here. Sweat cascaded down his face, so much that he had to keep shaking his head just to clear it from his eyes. And the searing heat only got worse the nearer he got to the pit at the end of the tunnel. Being careful not to slip, he craned his neck to look down at the bubbling, boiling furnace far below.

"What is that?" he whispered.

He heard LC clear his throat, a surefire warning sign of bad news. "The rock that the castle stands on forms the plug of a prehistoric volcano. The Black Lizard's digging must have, um, opened it up."

"And you're only telling me this NOW?" hissed Alfie.

In the Keep, Hayley covered the microphone. "You have to get him out of there!"

LC shook his head. "Not yet. We cannot allow the lizard to retrieve any more of the crown."

Alfie froze, trying not to make a sound. On the other side of the chasm, he could see the Black

Lizard's back, its cruel claws illuminated by the flames below. They were holding something up to the light. Alfie could see metal gleaming as the creature brushed away the dirt to reveal something golden.

A piece of Alfred the Great's ancient crown.

It had found it! Alfie was too late. The Black Lizard brought the newly found piece together with another fragment—this one larger, the half LC had feared the creature already possessed. In a flash of light, the two pieces fused as if magnetized, reforging themselves into one. Only a quarter of the crown remained missing. In its place, strange, twisted black bones bridged the gap.

"I can smell you, knight." The Black Lizard's voice was low and rasping.

Alfie steadied himself and held his ground, gripping his sword tighter. "What do you want?" He tried unsuccessfully to keep the tremble out of his voice.

"What is *mine*."

Flames shot up from the pit between them, sending a new wave of intense heat over Alfie. "It's not yours. I . . . I command you to put it down."

"Fool." The lizard's chuckle was loose and throaty. "No man commands me!"

The Black Lizard snapped its head around. It opened its mouth and launched a fireball toward

Alfie. There was no room to dodge the blast—Alfie took the blow full in his chest, and it sent him hurtling end over end, back into the tunnel.

It breathed fire! It breathed fire! Alfie thought as he tumbled over.

Voices barked across each other in his earpiece, but they were distant, dipping in and out. It was all Alfie could do to look up and focus on the large, dark shape that was crawling along the tunnel toward him.

Back at the Keep, everyone else could see it too.

"GET UP! ALFIE!" Hayley's voice came through loud and clear, screaming in his ear.

Alfie bent his knees, ignoring the burning pain from the hot scorch marks on his chest plate. He pointed his sword up and jumped. He crashed through the stone of the tunnel roof and back into the chapel, landing with a crunch on top of the upturned altar. He brought his sword around just as the floor exploded beneath him. Chunks of marble spewed in all directions as the Black Lizard burst upward, smashing a hole in the roof with its head, before landing again, pulverizing a wooden pew under its feet. Alfie could see it clearly now, but wished he couldn't. The fearsome lizard looked somehow even bigger up here. A slimy forked tongue flicked from between razor-sharp teeth, and vicious claws scraped against the stone floor as the beast stalked toward him. Energy fizzed off it, as strong as the heat that still pumped out from under their feet.

"I killed you once. What makes you think I won't do it again?" spat the Black Lizard.

Remembering something Brian had said in one of their late-night training sessions about attack being the best form of defense, Alfie launched himself from the altar, bringing the glowing sword down in an arc toward the lizard's neck.

Bad move. The creature casually whipped its tail around and swatted him with such power that Alfie was knocked sideways through the chapel wall, rolling to a halt in the rubble of the upper yard.

Seconds later the Black Lizard sprang out through the chapel roof and thudded down in the courtyard. The monster raised its powerful neck to the sky and belched more flame, amusing itself like a kid with a brand-new toy.

On his back, Alfie tried to crawl away. "Er, guys, I think our lizard might actually be a dragon. Repeat: THE LIZARD IS TURNING INTO A DRAGON!"

But no one replied. His camera and mic must have been offline. He was on his own. The Black Lizard—no, Black *Dragon*—leapt over and planted one great talon-tipped foot onto Alfie's chest, pinning him to the ground. Its dark, snakelike eyes gazed down at him, the deadly spiked tail weaving from side to side, ready to strike. *Was this the last thing my father saw?* Alfie wondered. No doubt he'd put up more of a fight. "Why are you doing this?"

The Black Dragon hesitated, as if thrown by the question. For a moment Alfie thought that he could feel the immense weight of the monster's foot lift from his chest—perhaps he was going to let him go after all.

"Destiny . . . ," sneered the Black Dragon. The hideous barbed tail stiffened, ready to pierce Alfie's chest plate and find his heart.

The earth lurched, throwing the Black Dragon off balance. The ground was rising and falling in waves beneath them. A strange sound rose up from the depths, like a thousand plugholes sucking down water all at once. Without warning, the Black Dragon turned and bounded away, clearing the far side of the castle walls in a single leap.

Alfie just had time to wonder what could have made it flee so suddenly when a huge crater opened up, swallowing the small chapel. Alfie scrambled backward as what was left of the castle tumbled into a giant sinkhole, the outer edges of the abyss expanding fast to within inches of his feet. It seemed to Alfie more like he was perched on the edge of some desolate mountain peak than a castle. No, not a mountain, more like . . . the lip of a volcano.

- TWENTY-ONE -

Eruption

The air turned crimson as a column of lava erupted from the sinkhole, shooting a hundred feet into the sky like a demented firework. Alfie recoiled from the blistering heat and threw himself off the battlements. Flames jetted from cracks in the cliff face, scorching his armor as he tumbled past, out of control. *Spurs, spurs, spurs!!* Wyvern sprang from his feet, emitting a high-pitched whinny of terror. She flew into action, dodging the fiery rocks that streaked past them like blazing meteorites.

Even through his helmet, Alfie could smell the sulfur fumes. A memory of a science lesson long ago and the sickly smell of rotten eggs popped into his head. He spotted a gap in the billowing black-and-red clouds that threatened to engulf them at any moment—a pinprick of clear sky. He pulled hard on Wyvern's reins until she spotted it too, and they streaked toward the closing gap. Bursting from the immense fireball, Alfie looked down at the city, and a thought flashed through his mind: *This must be what hell looks like.*

The volcano spewed lava and ash and huge black burning rocks in all directions. On one side, the cliff face of Edinburgh Castle had become a waterfall of fire, cascading into the park below. On the other, the lava flow was traveling the only way it could—down the hill of the Royal Mile. Buildings burst into flames one by one on either side of the narrow strip as the wall of lava rolled on, consuming cars, lampposts, and anything else in its path. People ran for their lives down the hill, screaming. But most terrifying of all was what Alfie could see from his position, hovering high above the street—the lava was getting faster.

The platoon of soldiers Alfie had seen at the castle gates was now running from house to house in front of the burning tide, pulling out any stragglers, shouting at them to move, almost hurling them down the street. Most didn't need to be told twice.

Alfie landed next to a soldier who was pounding on the door of a house. He wasn't very old, eighteen at most, with a face of ginger freckles smeared with sweat and soot. If he was surprised to see the Defender appearing in the middle of this chaos, he didn't show it—he had bigger things to worry about.

"I can't get any answer!" cried the soldier.

Alfie smashed his hand through the front

window and tossed in the Scout Orb. He watched as it whizzed through every room in the house and then shot back out into his waiting hand. "It's empty!" he said.

The soldier nodded and moved on.

Alfie sent the Orb through three more houses in quick succession—in the third he found an old man huddled behind a chair.

"Bottom right!" Alfie yelled, pointing at the house. Two soldiers broke in, carried the old man outside, and helped him down the hill.

More and more people were joining the exodus, running down the street, away from the tide of lava. But a bottleneck was forming at the bottom of the hill and panic was taking hold. Alfie looked back up the street. With nowhere else to go, the lava flow was still gaining speed, eating up everything in its path. He could summon Wyvern and start carrying people away two at a time, but that would take too long. He had to slow down the lava. Unsheathing his sword, Alfie began swinging at lampposts, felling them like trees. Sparks flew as they crashed onto the cobbles one by one. Blowing the sweat from his eyes, Alfie heaved the lampposts on top of each other across the road, forming a rudimentary dam. It worked.

"Ha, ha!" Alfie yelled, triumphant.

But then the lava simply squeezed through the gaps and around the sides, until finally it poured over the top and kept coming. The radio crackled back to life and he heard LC's frantic voice. "Majesty, Majesty! Where are you?"

"About ten seconds from being boiled alive."

In the Keep, Hayley was working to fix the feed from Alfie's camera. When it came back on the monitor, the lens was cracked, but they could see the lava flowing toward him.

"Get out of there!" barked Brian.

Alfie looked to the bottom of the hill. The crush was getting worse, as people clambered on top of each other to get away. "I can't! Not yet."

A large tourist bus was sitting abandoned. Alfie tried to push it around to block the road. Using the power of his armor, he edged the bus along inch by inch, but it wasn't fast enough.

"Have you tried looking for the keys?" shouted Hayley in his ears.

Good point, thought Alfie, feeling stupid. He ran to the bus and jumped in. Sure enough, the keys were still in the ignition—the driver must have left in a hurry. Firing up the engine, Alfie crunched the gears and swung the bus across the path of the lava flow. It wouldn't stop it, but he hoped it might slow it down.

The coach rocked as the lava buffeted the side. Alfie heard the wheels pop and the metal of the undercarriage begin to buckle. Time to leave. Flames rose up the doors—he wasn't getting out that way. Alfie unsheathed his sword and plunged it into the roof of the coach, carving a hole as fast as he could.

As he pulled himself out, he saw that the lava had simply picked the coach up and was pushing it downhill. Most of the pedestrians had now found shelter in one of the side streets, but a group of four soldiers were stranded on top of a car. The lava had them surrounded and was rising fast, already halfway up the doors.

Alfie summoned Wyvern from his spurs and made a beeline for them. He scooped one soldier, then another, up onto her back. She whinnied with the effort, but held her position, hovering over the car.

Alfie could see that he'd have no time to make a return trip for the other two. The lava was almost up to the roof. He had to take them now. Straining every muscle, Alfie lifted the third soldier, holding on to him with one hand and gripping Wyvern's reins tight with the other. The horse dipped, the weight pulling her within inches of the bubbling surface of the lava.

The last soldier—the freckle-faced young man Alfie had met farther up the street—screamed out for help. But Alfie couldn't release his grip on the soldier he was already holding, and he was scared to let go of Wyvern's reins, in case they all tumbled off.

"SAVE HIM!" the other soldiers yelled at Alfie.

But could they take the weight of another person? If Alfie didn't help the last soldier then he would be killed for sure; if he did, they might all die. A telegraph pole burst into flames next to them. Wyvern lurched backward and the pole just missed taking them all down with it. The horse groaned—she couldn't carry them all much longer. But now they were too far away to reach the last soldier. Lava was almost at the young man's feet. Alfie couldn't reach him in time. He'd hesitated too long and now he couldn't save him.

A beam of light from above dazzled Alfie for a moment. An RAF helicopter descended through the smoke. Wyvern carried the first three soldiers clear while a winchman zipped down a line at double speed from the chopper, plucking the last soldier off the car's roof just as it disappeared beneath the surface of the molten river.

Moments later, Alfie dropped the stunned soldiers off in a backstreet and then rode Wyvern up into the sky. Exhausted, he gazed down at Edinburgh. The heart of the city was in flames. It looked like a war zone.

The Lord Chamberlain's voice came over his earpiece. "Come home, Majesty."

Alfie steered them south. It felt like a retreat.

TWENTY-TWO

A Night Out

"My family and I wish to extend our sincere sympathies to the people of Scotland at this difficult time. The terrible events in Edinburgh have reminded us that we are all beholden to the power of Mother Nature . . . Sorry, I can't do this."

Alfie stopped reading, rubbed his eyes, and sat back in the chair at his father's desk. Correction: *his* desk. The king's desk. "Beholden? Who wrote this rubbish?"

"I did, Majesty." LC scowled at him from behind the camera.

The director kneaded his temples and ordered everyone to reset for another take. Their sixteenth. Technicians tinkered with the lights. A makeup lady rushed over and dabbed Alfie's face with a sponge. He could tell they were all just making a show of being busy while they waited for him to do a take without messing up. LC waved the makeup lady away and ushered Alfie into a quiet corner.

"Is there a problem, Majesty?"

"No . . . Yes! This stuff you've got me reading. It's ridiculous. It's not what I want to say."

"And what exactly *would* you like to say, sir?" asked LC.

Alfie couldn't shake the image of the terrified young soldier's face from his mind. Pleading for him to help. The look of horror when he realized he wasn't coming back for him. He wanted to find him, to explain that he was just a kid too, that he had been scared.

"I don't know. But something real, from the heart . . . How about 'sorry'? Sorry I was too weak to beat the Black Dragon. Sorry I couldn't stop half the city being burned to the ground. Sorry I wasn't brave enough to save that soldier."

LC looked around the room nervously, but no one had heard Alfie.

"The young man is fine. The helicopter picked him up," whispered LC.

"It should have been me!" snapped Alfie. "I need a break." Ignoring the Lord Chamberlain's disapproving frown, he stormed out.

• • •

Alfie found himself in the palace gardens. How many summer days had he spent exploring its warren of hedge-lined paths, herbaceous borders, and lakeside hideouts with Richard and Ellie when they were growing up? It felt like the whole world to him back then, an endless wilderness where he could roam free forever. Now he saw it for what it was: a garden surrounded by high walls, patrolled by guards, nothing but a mirage in the middle of a hostile desert.

He turned a corner and found Brian sitting on a bench.

"Blimey, can't I take a simple walk without you following me?" said Alfie.

"I wasn't. This is where I come to have my lunch." Brian held up a Tupperware box full of sandwiches and a banana. "But you can join me if you promise not to kill the mood."

Alfie slumped next to him on the bench. "Sorry."

"Still stewing over that Edinburgh mess, eh?"

Alfie nodded.

"You didn't run from the fight. That's all that matters," said Brian.

"It wasn't a fight. It was a beating! You didn't feel what it was like when the Black Dragon hit me—he's too strong."

"Maybe. But now we know he's only a man too—at least some of the time."

"How does that help if we have no way of finding out who he is?"

"I'm just saying, don't be too hard on yourself. You did fine out there."

"And next time, you'll do better." It was the Lord Chamberlain, stalking toward them between the flower beds. He continued: "After the coronation, when you are truly in command of your powers, you will be more of a match for that vile beast."

Coronation Day, thought Alfie. It was less than a week away. The day he would be officially crowned king. The day he would fully become the Defender—for life.

"The cameras await, Majesty . . ."

Alfie sighed and traipsed back inside to finish his broadcast.

"Would it kill you to give the boy some encouragement?" growled Brian, a few moments after he'd gone.

"I believe that is what I did," grumbled the Lord Chamberlain, affronted.

Brian started to stomp off, then changed his mind and turned back to fire off another salvo at the old man. "You remember when his father became king, don't you?"

"What an absurd question. Of course I do!"

"Then you remember how useless he was at first. He could hardly stand up straight in his armor without his knees knocking together. And the worst he had to face for the first year was a few grumpy marsh goblins."

"Ugh, the scourge of the Fens. Yes, I recall."

"So considering what Alfie's had thrown at him already, it's a miracle he's still in one piece."

"We're losing, you know." The Lord Chamberlain's face was lined with worry. "With each new fragment of the crown, our enemy is evolving, becoming *Drakonem*—a dragon. The first of its kind on these shores since the Great Fire. If we do not stop it, then we will have more than His Majesty's hurt feelings to worry about."

• • •

That evening, Alfie found Hayley alone in the Tower, fiddling with a laptop.

"Where is everyone?" asked Alfie as he stretched out next to Herne on the sofa. The dog woke up for a second, yawned, then fell asleep again.

"Playing hunt the clue downstairs." Hayley nodded toward the Archives. The Lord Chamberlain had everyone down there searching a thousand years' worth of secret scrolls and tomes, trying to uncover the hiding place of the final crown fragment.

Alfie watched Hayley tapping away at her keyboard. "Wi-Fi not working yet?"

Hayley shook her head. "You mean 'wee-fee,' remember?"

It was what LC insisted on calling it, and it usually made Alfie laugh. But not tonight.

Hayley turned around and saw his glum face. "Cheer up, Alfie—it was only a smackdown from a dragon supervillain and a major volcanic eruption. Apart from that, it was textbook."

Alfie laughed this time, but it was hollow. "It's not about me. It's about all those people out there. They deserve someone who can keep them safe."

"You're doing your best."

"What if my best isn't good enough?"

Hayley gazed over the laptop at Alfie, who was slouched on the old sofa like a rag doll. She shut down the computer. "Reckon you need a change of scene. My choice this time. Oh, but we'll need a ride."

Alfie shook his head. The last thing he wanted after the debacle in Edinburgh was to suit up again. But Hayley gave him one of her looks—she clearly wasn't going to leave him alone until he did what she wanted.

Moments later he slipped on the moth-eaten tunic and transformed into the Defender. Wyvern sprang out of his spurs and Alfie offered an armored gauntlet to Hayley, pulling her up behind him.

"OK, then. Where to?"

• • •

Turpin couldn't take much more of Fulcher's snoring. They had been sitting in their car outside the Whisper Grove Rest Home for over a week now, on the off chance that they might catch Hayley sneaking in to visit her gran. On day four they had agreed they were wasting their time. But the powers that be wanted them to wait . . . and wait . . . and wait. Turpin suspected they were being punished for failing to bag her the first time. But this was getting unpleasant now.

Stuff it, he thought. *She ain't coming.* He sneered at his partner, who was snorting and snuffling in her sleep like a hibernating bear. *If you can't beat 'em, join 'em.*

Turpin put his head back and closed his eyes. And precisely two seconds later a faint shaft of light shot through the sky above the car, disappearing somewhere behind the dark building.

• • •

"Gran . . . I want you to meet someone," said Hayley.

Alfie had taken off the tunic when they landed in the dark garden. It was way past visiting hours, but luckily Hayley's gran's ground-floor room backed onto the garden. It had been a simple matter to pry open the window and climb inside.

Alfie shook the old woman's hand. "I'm Alfie. Pleased to meet you."

"Knock me down with a feather," Hayley's gran said. "You look just like that young Prince of Wales."

Alfie and Hayley shared an amused glance.

"Um, Gran, he *is*. Well, he was. He's king now."

The old woman burst out laughing. "Pull the other one, Hales!" But then she stopped, puzzled, when she saw they weren't joining in. She looked Alfie up and down more closely, then flew into action, guiding her new motorized wheelchair to a mirror and brushing her hair. "How do you know each other? Do you go to the same school?"

"Hayley's been working at the palace," said Alfie.

"Yeah, IT mainly. Pretty boring. Place is stuck in the Dark Ages."

"Look at me in my dressing gown with my hair like a bird's nest, honestly. Sorry, Your Majesty," said Hayley's gran. "Oh, Lordy. Let me rustle up some tea!"

Without warning she reversed the wheelchair over Alfie's foot before he could jump out of the way. She spun the chair around and reached for a button on a wall to call a nurse. But Hayley stepped in front of her.

"No tea, thanks, Gran. Why don't we just have a chat?"

And chat they did. Hayley's gran reveled in telling Alfie all about her "nice hotel" and how much better the food was here than when Hayley was cooking for her. Hayley didn't rise to the bait; she was just happy to see her looking so well. She giggled as Gran showed off her Union Jack tea towels and commemorative mug collection from the last two coronations to Alfie. It turned out she'd even slept out on the streets of London the night before Alfie's dad was crowned king, so that she got a good spot to watch the procession go by.

"I expect you were too little to remember much of that, Your Majesty."

Alfie laughed. "Just call me Alfie, please."

Gran smiled and nodded. "Suppose that makes you King Alfred the Second. Blow me sideways, you've got a lot to live up to, sweetheart."

Alfie's smile faded. "Yeah, I know."

Hayley wondered if they should get going before he spun off into another bad mood. But before she could say anything, her gran had taken Alfie's hand in hers. "Let me look at you." The old woman stared deep into the young king's eyes, sizing him up. "It's only natural to feel scared. You're so young. It's like when I first drove a Tube train on my own. There was little old me, with all these carriages full of people rattling around behind. Their lives were in my hands and they didn't even know it! It was a big responsibility for a young girl, all lonely and afraid down there in the dark. But as we came out of the tunnel into the fresh air at White City station, do you know what happened?"

Alfie shook his head. The old lady shot up from her wheelchair, arms wide.

"The sun came blazing out of a clear blue sky. I'd led everyone out of the night and into the light! Hallelujah!"

"Hallelujah!" cried Hayley, throwing her arms into the air too.

"Hallelujah," Alfie added to the chorus and joined in the laughter.

A sharp *rat-a-tat-tat* at the door made them all jump.

"Everything all right, Mrs. Hicks?" It was one of the nurses.

Alfie dived under the bed and Hayley leapt into the bathroom as the door opened and the nurse stuck her head into the room.

"Oh, yes, my love. I'm just talking to the King of England." Gran beamed.

The nurse nodded gravely. "I'll go and get your medicine." She shut the door and hurried off. Alfie climbed out from under the bed and Hayley emerged from the bathroom, snickering.

"We'd better go," said Hayley, guiding her gran back into bed.

Her gran frowned at Alfie. "Aren't you going to introduce me to your friend first?"

Hayley sighed and kissed her on the cheek. "Maybe next time, OK? Night, night."

Gran settled back in her bed, singing to herself as Hayley and Alfie climbed out of the window. "Good-bye-ee, good-bye-ee, wipe the tear, baby dear, from your eye-ee . . ."

They didn't say anything to each other until they were back on Wyvern, rising out of the garden.

"Sorry about that," Hayley called out. "She gets confused. I think she got a kick out of meeting you, though. Thanks for taking me."

"No problem," replied Alfie. "I was honored to meet her. She's quite a lady."

"Yes, she is," said Hayley.

She wrapped her arms around the Defender's waist and hunkered down. As they sailed over the roof of the old people's home, she thought she saw a familiar-looking car sitting across the street with two figures slouched in the front. "Mind if we take a quick detour, Alfie?"

• • •

Thunder boomed all around Turpin and Fulcher, waking them with a start and sending them tumbling out onto the road. Puzzled, they sprang up and looked all around for the source of the terrible racket. Then they noticed the roof of their car. It was covered in deep dents—hoof-shaped dents.

TWENTY-THREE

Next in Line

"This is . . . unacceptable! *Unacceptable!*"

Alfie and Hayley were sitting at the ops table, while LC paced around, fuming. His normally pallid skin was pricked with red. Nearby, Brian leaned against an ancient pillar, managing to scowl as he went at his teeth with a toothpick. Yeoman warders scurried around looking busy, but Alfie could tell they were listening as their king was given the mother of all tellings-off.

"LC, it's fine. No one saw us," Alfie said.

"You don't know that," Brian said. "Ever since Edinburgh the country is going Defender crazy."

It was true: The Defender had been snapped by camera phones more than once as he tried to divert the lava on the Royal Mile. Nothing conclusive, but too many people had seen him there for it to be dismissed as a hoax this time. The overexcited media was now talking around the clock about "the superhero in our midst" and who it could be. And people were sending in pictures nonstop: weather balloons, Chinese lanterns, and really bright stars in the sky; anything and everything was now being mistaken for the Defender.

"As for you, young lady," lectured LC, turning his fire on Hayley, "you're still wanted for questioning by MI5! How do you know they're not watching your grandmother's care home, waiting for you to visit? The fact that you two weren't recognized or caught is just . . . blind luck!"

Alfie and Hayley shared a silent look. Probably best not to mention their little good-bye present for the secret-agent goons, then.

"An unauthorized Defender mission!? What if something had happened? We had no idea where you were! There is no way we could have sent help!"

"I'm Defender of the Realm. I'm not supposed to need help!" Alfie shouted, storming off.

He was under enough pressure without being scolded like a naughty schoolboy. He stalked down a passageway, feeling miserable. He didn't know where he was heading and he just let the warren of hallways take him deeper and deeper into the Keep, past old storerooms with heavy iron doors and an armory, its metal racks full of neatly stowed pikes and swords. Another door led into a large dormitory with a barrel roof. The place seemed deserted, so Alfie walked in, curious. Immaculately made bunk beds ran down both sides, with footlockers beside them. It must have been where the yeoman warders slept when they were off duty.

Alfie picked up a framed photograph next to one of the beds. It was funny to see the burly, bearded yeoman warder out of his uniform, but here he was, posing with his two kids on a beach somewhere, without a care in the world.

"Lord alive, the guvnor's in a right stinker tonight."

Voices in the corridor, coming his way. Alfie put the photograph down and ducked behind a bunk bed. He had every right to be here, of course, but somehow he still felt like he was trespassing. A pair of yeoman warders trudged in, pulling off their hats and tossing them onto their bunks, which were thankfully some ways away. Alfie recognized one of them: He was the Ravenmaster, in charge of looking after the Tower's ravens when he wasn't in the Keep.

"Bit hard on the lad, I thought," said the Ravenmaster, unbuttoning his tunic. "Remember that time his old dad had a row with the missus and took Wyvern on a joy ride over the Atlantic to get her back?"

The other yeoman warder's laugh was gruff and warm. "Yeah, thought the boss was going to blow a fuse when he found out! Maybe the lad's a chip off the old block after all."

Alfie smiled, thinking maybe he should step out of his hiding place and make a joke about being there.

"Still, can't help wondering what the spare would have been like," said the other beefeater. The two men walked past Alfie's hiding place without even glancing in his direction and headed for another room that held rows of old-fashioned porcelain baths.

"How'd you mean?" asked the Ravenmaster, turning a brass tap on.

"Richard. Seems more like king material if you ask me."

"Statement of the bloomin' obvious, Terry," replied the Ravenmaster. "Still, ours is not to reason why; ours is but to do and die."

"Problem is, with that skinny lad in the suit, we might just be doing and dying sooner rather than later."

The Ravenmaster slammed the door to the bathroom, and Alfie could hear their muffled laughter. His heart sank. *They don't think I can do it. I'm not up to the job. I'm not smart enough. I'm not strong enough. I'm just not . . . enough.*

He wasn't even angry. How could he be, when deep down he knew that they were right? He had known it ever since the first night he'd come to the Keep and learned about his family's incredible secret. He'd known it when he struggled through training and on his first outings as the Defender. He'd known it on that terrible night in Edinburgh when a brave young man looked to him for help and he came up short. But what could he do about it?

I am the master of my fate, I am the captain of my soul . . .

The words of the poem Professor Lock had quoted to him at the coronation rehearsal swirled around his head. This was *his* life, *his* decision. He wasn't cut out to be the king, let alone the Defender of the Realm. Never was. Never would be.

But I know someone who is.

• • •

Richard weaved past one player, floored another with his shoulder, and shoved a third hard in the chest, sending him toppling backward. He sold the fullback a dummy, pretending to pass to one of his teammates, and crossed the line at an easy trot, placing the rugby ball down as cheers erupted from the spectators. But rather than celebrate, Richard walked straight back to the last player he'd pushed over and offered him his hand, pulling him back to his feet.

No one noticed Alfie sitting some ways off in the shade of a tree. He had instructed Brian that this would be a discreet, unofficial visit. Brian was burning to know why they were back at Harrow, but Alfie had only told him it wouldn't take long— he just needed to speak to his brother. As the teams trudged back toward the changing rooms, Richard spotted Alfie, flashed a surprised smile, and jogged over. He didn't even look tired.

"Hey, bro. Saw your speech on the news last night. How mental was that Edinburgh thing? Ellie keeps saying it was all to do with superheroes again. They'll send her off to the loony bin if she's not careful."

"She's actually pretty smart, you know."

Richard frowned at Alfie. They'd always been able to read each other's moods. Secrets never lasted long between twins. "Something you want to get off your chest, Alf?"

Alfie checked that no one was in earshot. Brian had kept his distance, as instructed. "It's more of a request, actually . . . I was wondering if you'd do me a favor." This was harder than he'd expected.

"Spit it out then, Alfie, I'm noxious," Richard said, sniffing his armpit and pulling a face. "Need to hit the showers."

"OK, then. You know you said to call if I needed anything? Well, I do . . . I want you to be king. Instead of me. Please."

Richard laughed. Then he looked at Alfie's

exhausted and somber face. "What? But . . . you can't do that."

"Actually, I can. It's called abdication. It's unusual, but it's happened before."

Alfie had never seen Richard lost for words. For a moment he thought his brother was going to throw up. But as they walked around the playing fields, Alfie laid out his case, why he wasn't up to the task . . . and the solid reasons why Richard was.

"I'm just not like you. People don't want to follow me. But they'll follow you."

"But, Alfie," spluttered Richard, "think of everything you're asking me to give up. They wouldn't let me play sports anymore. I could forget my army career. My life would be over!"

"I know, Rich, and I'm sorry," said Alfie. He had left his best argument for last. "But I think it's what Dad would have wanted. You can't say it's not true."

They were both in tears.

"The country needs you, Rich, more than you know."

The only thing Alfie didn't talk about was the other side to the job: being the Defender. He knew that if he did, Richard would just think he'd lost his mind. Flying horses, magic armor, and Black Dragons—that was stuff Richard was just going to have to learn about the hard way. Alfie had no doubt his brother would handle it better than he had.

. . .

"You can't, Majesty!"

Alfie marveled at how the Lord Chamberlain was still using the formal "Majesty," despite the fact that he looked like he was about to have a heart attack.

"I wish people would stop telling me what I can and can't do!" shouted Alfie. "None of this was my idea, in case you've forgotten. You dumped all this on me before my father's body was even cold!"

"But . . . But . . . But . . . ABDICATION?" stammered LC. "It is a dereliction of your responsibility! An affront to every tradition we hold dear! Sir, you are the king. You are Defender of the Realm. You are duty-bound to . . . think of your *country*! Think of your *people*!"

"THAT'S WHAT I'M TRYING TO DO!" It was Alfie's final word. He stormed out of the Keep, closely followed by Hayley.

Brian, who had been listening, eased himself onto the sofa with a deep sigh. "I warned you. I said if you kept pushing him . . ."

But LC didn't answer. He leaned heavily on the ops table, head bowed, a haunted look in his eyes.

Alfie was still fuming when he reached the underground carriage. "'Think of your country!' Can you believe he said that to me? At least I won't have to listen to his stupid lectures anymore."

"Yeah," said Hayley. "Thing is, though, the old geezer's right."

Alfie turned to her in disbelief. "You actually AGREE with him?"

"Yeah, I do," she said. "You can't bail now just because one fight went a bit pear-shaped."

"It's not just that. It's been like this my whole life. Everyone looking at me, judging me, telling me how I have to do my duty. I don't expect you to understand. You're not even . . ."

"Not what? A royal?! You think just 'cause I wasn't born with a silver spoon in my mouth, I don't know about doing my duty? I've done more for my family than you've ever done for yours. Run away if you want to, but do me a favor: Don't pretend this is about anything else besides you being a coward."

"OK! I admit it! I'm scared! I'm scared that I can't beat that thing! I'm scared I won't be able to save anyone! I'm scared of turning into my father—a miserable, lonely failure!"

Hayley was shaking; there were tears in her eyes. "I saw your dad fight, and he was brave and he was loyal and he never gave up. So don't worry about that—you're nothing like him." Still trembling with rage, she turned and walked away.

• • •

Hours later, Richard still sat where his brother had left him, out on the dark playing fields of Harrow. He didn't notice the cold wind whipping past. He didn't hear the teacher calling his name up at the school. All he felt was an odd rushing sensation, like his own pulse throbbing in his head. Shadows seemed to dance in the mist over the rugby pitch as if they were alive, searching for something. His fingers tingled as he picked at a scab on his knee. He winced in pain and looked down, shaken from his daydream. Blood was running down his leg.

Thick, blue blood.

- TWENTY-FOUR -

Unconquered

Alfie never thought he'd be so happy to see the prison again. After everything he'd been through, passing back through the gates of Harrow School suddenly felt more like arriving on break. His old room with its bare walls seemed warm and welcoming. As he sat at his desk, looking out across the rooftops, he let out a deep sigh of relief.

"Where do you want these, then?" asked a low, monotone voice from his doorway.

It was Jim or Jeff, his new bodyguard—Alfie couldn't remember his name—lugging his suitcases inside. With Brian now reassigned to Richard, Alfie had landed a shuffling mess in a baggy suit. If Brian was all cut and chiseled Special Forces, then Jim or Jeff was more the Special Chip-Frying Unit of the Army Catering Corps. Protecting the young, failed ex-king was clearly not deemed an especially important job these days.

"Anywhere you like," Alfie answered.

Jim or Jeff took him at his word, tossing the

cases into the middle of the floor. He shuffled off, mumbling something about putting the kettle on.

Alfie could feel the stress of the last few days lifting from his shoulders already. When the news had broken about his abdication, the newspapers and TV commentators, far from giving him credit for seeing sense and handing over the reins to Richard—something they'd been calling for him to do for weeks—had instead savaged him like a pack of hounds. *Turncoat. Deserter. Traitor.* Those were some of the nicer labels they had thrown at him. He was "sullying his father's memory" by abandoning his duty before it had even begun, according to the critics. Alfie had tried to ignore it as much as he could.

Ellie had been furious with him, of course—she yelled down the phone that he had ruined Richard's life. Why couldn't he just go through the motions and do the job? Was it really that hard? What else was he going to do all day? Alfie longed to tell her his real reasons, but he didn't want to betray LC's trust in him any more than he had already.

But it was Hayley he still felt most guilty about. His decision meant that she was going back to her gran's empty flat with nothing to do but wait for social services to collect her.

The Lord Chamberlain generously offered to let Hayley stay—she'd earned a place in the Keep. But as touched as she was, Hayley could see that the team was breaking up and it wouldn't be the same. Besides, she said, if the Black Dragon was going to win and the world was about to get as "Dark Age-y" as they all thought, then she should spend as much time with her gran as she could. Alfie had texted her to say sorry and good luck, but she hadn't replied.

Had she been right about him? Alfie wondered. Was he making excuses? Was he persuading himself he was stepping aside for the greater good when really he was just a coward? Alfie shook his head and opened the window to air out the room. He had to stop beating himself up like this. *He* knew why he'd done it. It was the right call. He hoped that wherever his father was, he knew that too.

No one at school treated Alfie any differently. The rugby team was annoyed at losing their star player, but most of the boys left him alone to settle back into the daily routine.

Except, of course, for Mortimer. He was like a cat with an injured bird—he planned on torturing Alfie for the rest of his school life and was making no secret of the fact. And yet something very important had changed since their last fateful meeting in the library. Alfie had faced far scarier monsters than some mere school bully; he'd been in real danger, fought in real battles (even if he had lost and been thrown through a wall). So when Mortimer approached him in the dining hall on that first evening back, spilling his tray of food all over him and kicking his chair away, Alfie found there was something missing. Something that had always been there before, but now was gone. Fear.

"Poor little Princess." Mortimer was practically paralyzed with laughter as he stood over him.

Alfie stood up, plucked a slice of pizza off the floor, and pushed it very slowly and deliberately into Mortimer's face. For a moment the big thug was too stunned to react. Every boy in the hall sucked in a sharp breath, waiting for the beating that was surely coming Alfie's way. But when Mortimer swung his hulking fist at his face, Alfie ducked, spun on his heel, and knocked Mortimer off balance with one sweep of his leg. Those nights of training with Brian hadn't gone to waste. The moves were part of his muscle memory now. Mortimer roared like an angry bear, scooped up a fork from the table, and jabbed it at Alfie's neck. But Alfie deflected the blow and used Mortimer's own weight against him, heaving him onto the table and sliding him through a dozen half-eaten suppers, before finally crashing into a humiliating heap in the corner. Mortimer hadn't even looked at Alfie since.

Alfie smiled as he sat in his room and listened to the rain drumming against the window. School had broken up early that weekend to allow students to travel home and be with their families for the coronation. But he would stay here, alone—well, apart from Jim or Jeff, who seemed to mainly sleep and worry about whether the snack machine down the corridor would run out of chips.

But Alfie didn't mind. All he wanted was for everything to go well for his brother. There had been no sign of the Black Dragon since Edinburgh. Maybe the creature had returned to whatever vile place it had slithered out of. Maybe King Richard would be able to enjoy some peace while he got a grip on his new double role. And Alfie would be there for him when he wanted to talk about it—a confidant, an ally, a shoulder to cry on if he needed it. Though, knowing Richard, Alfie doubted he would.

But for now, Alfie had a ton of schoolwork to catch up on. He still owed Professor Lock a history essay, but his teacher hadn't been at school when Alfie returned. Alfie was sad not to see him. He'd wanted to thank him for his support, for showing him an escape route out of the mess he'd found himself in. But Lock had been called to the palace to help tutor Richard and wouldn't be back until after the coronation.

He had, however, left Alfie something on the desk in his room—a copy of the poem he'd quoted in the Abbey. It was called "Invictus." Alfie flicked through his Latin dictionary and found the word. It meant "Unconquered."

- TWENTY-FIVE -

Coronation Day

They'd been stopping her from seeing Richard all morning ("Too busy," "Final preparations," "Just give him some space, Your Highness"), but now Princess Eleanor had run out of patience. Telling the footman guarding the door that she would start screaming and wouldn't stop until he moved, Ellie finally made it into the king's dressing room. Richard hadn't heard her come in. He was standing in front of a mirror, looking very smart in his naval cadet's dress uniform. His sleeve was rolled up and he seemed to be staring at the veins in his wrists.

"You OK, Ricky?" Ellie always called him that when she was feeling playful.

Richard whipped his sleeve down, fixing the cuff links. "Ellie. Hi." But his smile couldn't disguise the dark bags under his eyes or the frown lines etched into his forehead.

"What's wrong?" she asked.

Silly question. It would be a little weird if her brother were not nervous. He'd only just found out he was going to be king and was about to be crowned

in front of a worldwide TV audience of billions, after all.

"I just feel kind of . . . strange. Like I shouldn't really be here."

"Well, that's 'cause you shouldn't."

Ellie mentally kicked herself. She'd told herself to stay positive and not stir up an argument—it had lasted all of ten seconds, as usual. Richard took her by the shoulders and fixed her with a firm-but-kind stare. Maybe it was just the uniform, but he looked like he'd aged about ten years since she last saw him.

"Don't blame Alfie," said Richard. "None of this is his fault. And maybe he's right. Maybe it's better this way . . ."

Ellie nodded. There was no point in getting angry on Richard's big day. She hugged him tightly, burying her face against the rough fabric of his jacket.

From the window, Richard could see police dogs performing one last sweep of the Mall, checking for explosives. Steel barriers had been erected for days, ready to hold back the crowds from the road.

"Do you think they'll come?" Richard asked.

"Who?" asked Ellie.

"The people."

. . .

They did. By car, by train, by coach, and by foot. From tower blocks, from towns and villages, from every corner of the country and beyond, people came to see the new king crowned. Whether out of curiosity, or old-fashioned patriotism, the quiet masses would make their presence felt today. By early morning they were ten deep at the barriers lining the route from Buckingham Palace to Westminster Abbey. Flags from all over the world, not just the Union Jack, were held high. In streets and living rooms all over Britain, there was a party atmosphere. News reporters were quick to label it the "Richard Effect"—people had come out to support the humble young man who never wanted the throne, but had bravely accepted the responsibility from his feckless twin. But there was more to it than that. This was one of those days when history became more than just a dusty pile of books in a library. It was a living thing, happening in front of their eyes, and no one, not even the hardest cynic, wanted to miss that.

Alfie, by contrast, was hidden away in his bedroom at school. He had decided not to watch the TV coverage. Instead he'd tried to take his mind off it by finishing his history essay. He was up at seven a.m., putting the finishing touches to it and spell-checking. But as he passed the staff room on his way to deliver it to Professor Lock's study, he caught sight of Jim or Jeff slouched in front of the television, munching through a huge bowl of cheesy puffs while he watched the buildup to the live coronation broadcast. The Gold State Coach with its eight horses was waiting at the palace gates for the young King Richard to emerge. There was a phalanx of Grenadier Guards behind it, as well as a detachment of Blues and Royals on horseback, their armor flashing bright in the sun. Closest to the coach, forming a protective ring around it, were the yeoman warders in their red dress uniform, garlands of flowers around their Tudor hats.

"Hur, hur, hur, look at those prats," grunted Jim or Jeff.

If only you knew, thought Alfie. On TV the commentators were describing the route the coach would take: down the Mall, past St. James's Park, under Admiralty Arch, down the long stretch through Whitehall, past Big Ben and the Palace of Westminster, before finally delivering Richard to the grand porch of Westminster Abbey. Alfie wondered how his brother was feeling right now. He wondered how *he* would have felt, if he'd chosen to stay. The thought made his stomach lurch. No, he couldn't watch. Alfie moved on, through the hallways of the deserted school.

The study door was locked. Alfie had planned to leave the essay for his teacher to find on his return—he wanted him to be impressed at how fast he had thrown himself back into his studies. Alfie had even added a note to the front, thanking Professor Lock for the poem (*Turns out I am the captain of my soul after all! Or at least a lance corporal*). He knelt down and tried to slide the essay underneath the door. But the gap was too narrow and it kept scuffing the pages. Alfie was annoyed— he didn't want to ruin his work after he'd made so much effort. He rested a hand on the door handle, trying one more time, but the thick wad of stapled pages wouldn't go under. *Come on!*

Clunk. He felt the handle flush hot for a moment in his hand, and the door popped ajar. His fingertips tingled with a familiar sensation. His veins pulsed faint blue. *Guess I've still got a little of the old magic left in me. At least for another hour or so*, Alfie thought, and stepped inside.

Thin blades of light sliced through the closed shutters. It was just enough for Alfie to pick his way past the precarious piles of books that were dotted around the floor, overspill from the fully stuffed floor-to-ceiling bookshelves, as he edged toward the professor's desk. Compared with the rest of the room, the desk looked almost unused. A couple of framed photos and a pen were all that occupied it. There wasn't even a computer. Alfie felt weird, trespassing in someone else's personal space. He didn't want to hang around in here, so he placed the essay on the desk and headed for the door.

Wait, what's that going to look like? Like he broke in just to deliver his essay. Lock would think he was some kind of psycho. No, he'd put it on the floor on the way in, like he'd managed to slide it under the door after all. Alfie scooped up the pages, but as he did so, he knocked one of the framed photos over. Cursing his clumsiness, he picked it up and checked for damage. No cracks—phew.

Then he focused in on the picture itself—a cheerful Lock, surrounded by a gaggle of students wearing waterproof jackets. Lock had his metal detector slung over his shoulder like a rifle, and he was standing by some kind of freshly excavated pit. But there was something else in the background—something Alfie recognized—a large chalk figure carved into the hillside.

The Westbury White Horse.

A strange, cold sensation crept up his spine, like ice crystals forming on a windowpane. What was it that LC had said about the White Horse? It was the site of the battle in which Alfred the Great had defeated the Vikings; mysterious holes had appeared there the previous summer; it was where the Black

Dragon must have found the very first piece of Alfred's crown. Alfie put the picture down and started to scour the cramped study more carefully. He didn't know what he was looking for exactly, but he had to know if there was even the slightest possibility that the crazy idea beginning to form in his head could be true.

Was it Professor Lock who had found the original piece of Alfred's lost crown? Could his teacher be the Black Dragon?

But there was nothing else in the study to suggest Lock had anything to do with the creature—no photographs, no documents. Alfie was relieved; maybe it was just a coincidence. And yet there was that cold feeling tiptoeing over his skin again, like some deep animal alarm, sensing danger. A sheet of paper—the note that had been attached to the front of his essay—was moving on the desk, lifting ever so slightly off the wood, rippling, as if blown by a draft. He picked it up and leaned down, putting his face to the desk. He could feel air coming through a tiny hole in the wood. But how? He crawled around the desk, looking for a gap, but there was nothing. The desk was built into grooves in the floor; he couldn't even move it.

Alfie sat down in the deep leather chair, perplexed. He tried to pick up the single pen that lay on the desk, but only one end of it moved, lifting upward like a hinge. Without warning, the entire desk slid backward with a soft *whir* and the chair he was sitting in glided down through the floor.

The chair jolted to a halt, and Alfie saw that he was sitting at the center of a large subterranean chamber. It was cold and musty, like the wine cellar his father had once shown him under the palace kitchens. Mounted on thick, wooden brackets on the wall were huge bones—backbones mainly, black and jagged like a giant millipede's skeleton had been coiled several times around the room. Whatever this creature once was, it had been huge. The tight, snaking bundle of bones ended at an enormous, heavy skull, lined with dagger-long teeth. Alfie gasped as he realized that the lizard-like creature also had wings, which hung in heavy, rotted tatters from the ceiling. There was only one thing it could be.

A dragon.

Alfie felt like he might be sick. But it was undeniable: Professor Lock must have found the pieces of King Alfred's crown and, using its power-ful magic, transformed himself into the Black Dragon. Alfie thought back to everything Lock had told him about finding his own path, his own destiny. His teacher had been whispering poison into his ear, encouraging him to step aside, throw-ing the Succession into crisis just when the

Defender was needed most. Was he now doing the same to Richard? What did he have planned for Alfie's brother? What would happen to him when Lock found the final piece of Alfred's crown?

Alfie noticed a large map of the United Kingdom pinned to the wall beneath the dragon's skeleton. It was annotated with tightly scrawled notes, some of them scratched out, others underlined. Crosses were drawn over dozens of locations, many of which Alfie had visited himself in his search for the fragments of Alfred's crown. Only four had thick circles drawn around them: Westbury, Stonehenge, Edinburgh Castle, and . . . Alfie shuddered.

"Oh no . . ."

Westminster Abbey.

- TWENTY-SIX -

Get Me to the Abbey on Time

"Is this seat taken?"

Professor Lock smiled graciously as he eased himself into a pew next to a rather large lady wearing a wide-brimmed, peach-colored hat. Westminster Abbey had never looked so resplendent. Every inch of gold and silver shone bright. The checkered marble floor sparkled, and swathes of red velvet cascaded from the balconies above the expectant congregation. Lock loved this place. And yet he doubted that the other guests, fussing with their ties and hats and reading their programs for the tenth time, realized that beneath the vaulted ceilings and towering columns, what they were really surrounded by was death. The bones and ashes of kings, queens, priests, and poets lay interred in the stone all around them. These ancient walls would see more death before the day was out, of that he was certain.

Lock slid his hand into his waistcoat pocket and felt for the smooth, pebble-sized object sewn into the seam. It had been easy to smuggle it through the metal detectors operated by the dozy police officers at the entrance. Even if they had found it, would they have recognized what it was? A dull, green emerald of average size, just one more jewel amid a sea of gems twinkling from hundreds of necks and hands today. They couldn't possibly have known it was part of Alfred the Great's original crown, the relic Lock was so close to reassembling for the first time in a thousand years. And when he did . . . Well, there would be time for that later. Now he had work to do.

The emerald would tell him when it was close to the final piece of the lost crown, wherever it was hidden. It had led him the same way to the fragments at Stonehenge and Edinburgh Castle, pulling like a magnet, yearning to be reunited. He had tried to find the last piece once before, during the coronation rehearsal, but the Abbey was a big place and he had run out of time. However, more research had yielded a clue—like arrows pointing the way. Now he was sure he knew where to look. He just had to get close enough at the right moment.

Lock slipped out of his seat and made his way toward a shadowy alcove. He had dedicated his life to studying history, but today he would be making it. Soon there would be a new ruler of these islands. Soon the kingdom would kneel before a new master.

. . .

Alfie was close to panic. He had to talk to Brian and the Lord Chamberlain. He needed to warn them. Richard was walking into a trap. The Black Dragon—Lock!—was waiting for him, and for all Alfie knew, he might have the final piece of Alfred's crown in his possession already.

"I don't understand it—why isn't Brian answering his phone?" asked Alfie, frustrated.

"I told you, sir," replied Jim or Jeff, flustered by having to interrupt his chip-eating. "The Abbey is locked down for the coronation—all mobile devices checked at the door. But if you'd care to give me a message, I could try to get it to him after the ceremony . . ."

Alfie glanced at the TV and saw his brother walking out of the palace and stepping into the Gold State Coach. He prayed the yeoman warders could protect him. But how could they when they had no idea what was coming?

"You need to take me to the Abbey."

The flabby bodyguard almost choked on his cheesy puffs and proceeded to list the reasons why this would be impossible. No one was expecting Alfie; there would be no security team in place; he'd sort of promised he wouldn't go, so it was bound to cause a fuss. Plus traffic into town would be murder. It was no use; Jim or Jeff clearly wasn't going to help him. Alfie forced a smile and apologized, making an excuse about the pressure of the day getting to him, and walked out. He bounded up the stairs to his room. There was one other person he could try.

He just hoped she was still talking to him.

• • •

Hayley was in her bedroom at her gran's flat, zipping the last of her clothes into an old suitcase. In the living room, Sandra, her perky social worker, was perched on the sofa watching the coronation on TV.

"Hayley, you should see this! The new king's on his way!" she shouted.

Hayley lugged the case out of her room. Sandra had arrived earlier that morning to get her. She'd asked lots of questions about where Hayley had been the past few weeks, but Hayley hadn't told her anything.

"Ready when you are." Hayley dropped her case down and stood in front of the TV.

"Don't you want to watch this?" Sandra asked, craning her neck to see the screen. "It's history."

Hayley shook her head. "Nah. Not really my thing."

Outside the tower block, Hayley carried her suitcase past Dean Barron and his mates, who were clustered around his lime-green Peugeot hatchback, cranking bass-heavy hip-hop out of the oversized speakers.

"Don't forget to write!" Dean shouted to her, snickering.

"Just ignore him," Sandra said helpfully.

Hayley's phone buzzed in her pocket. She fished it out and her heart skipped a beat—IRON EAGLE flashed up on the screen. Hayley answered, but the beats from Dean's stupid car were so loud, she had to strain to hear what Alfie was saying. He was both jabbering too fast and whispering—not a great combo. Something about the Black Dragon, the Abbey, terrible danger. One thing was clear— he needed help, and fast.

Hayley made a snap decision. "Hey, Dean?" The boy racer had just enough time to look up at her before he caught the full weight of Hayley's suitcase in his stomach as she swung it forward, knocking him over. Hayley jumped into the Peugeot and cranked the ignition.

"Alfie? Be there before you know it," she shouted into the phone before hanging up and slamming the car door closed.

Sandra was running toward the car, shouting and waving her arms, but Hayley threw the hatchback into reverse, over-revved the engine, and shot backward, mounting the curb with a loud crunch.

Now Dean was running at her too. "Please don't hurt my car! Please don't hurt my car!"

He was actually crying.

Hayley ground the gears and shot forward, speeding past him. Soon all she could see in the rearview mirror was a shocked Sandra staring after her, while Dean jumped up and down, screaming like a toddler. It was an image she would treasure for years to come.

• • •

I seriously need to invest in a rope ladder, thought Alfie as he lost his grip on the drainpipe and fell into the flower bed outside his bedroom window.

As far as he knew, Jim or Jeff was none the wiser. He was probably still slumped in front of the TV, stuffing his face. But just as Alfie leapt over the low wall onto the street, he found himself face-to-face with his startled bodyguard, who was paying a pizza delivery guy. Luckily for Alfie, his reactions were faster. He streaked past, and by the time the lumbering bodyguard had carefully placed his pizza box down and taken up the chase, Alfie had a healthy head start. Mind you, he wasn't going to get that far unless Hayley came through . . .

SCREEEEECH!

A lime-green Peugeot veered onto the sidewalk and stopped about an inch from his legs. Hayley poked her head over the steering wheel and took her hand off her eyes. She beamed, evidently pleased she hadn't hit him.

"OI! COME BACK!"

Jim or Jeff was wheezing down the hill toward them, with what was left of his career flashing before his eyes.

Alfie ducked into the passenger seat. "Nice wheels. Drive!"

The road was quiet at first, which was good because Hayley liked to use *all* of it. She tried to reassure Alfie that she'd driven a car before, although that was in a car park, for about five minutes, and she'd still managed to hit a post. The GPS barked directions as they sped into Central London.

"You *don't* want to be king. You *do* want to be king. Make up your mind, mate!" yelled Hayley over the angry beeping of car horns.

"It's not that," said Alfie. "But what you said before—you were right. I chickened out and ran away and now Richard's in danger and it's all my fault."

"Still, I was out of order," replied Hayley. "You were doing your best. I wouldn't want to be a princess in a million years—"

Alfie pointed, alarmed. "Car, car, CAR!"

He squeezed his eyes shut as Hayley swerved around a slow-moving car in front of them, tires screeching.

"Maybe we should talk about it later?" gasped Alfie, as the GPS told them to make a U-turn, which Hayley did, narrowly missing a tree.

"You might be dead later, especially if the Black Dragon's really there."

"Yeah, unless your driving kills me first!"

They just had to get close enough to the Abbey for Alfie to reach his brother, but they couldn't afford any delays. They might be traveling faster than Richard's horse-drawn carriage, but he was supposed to be on the roads and they weren't.

"Diversion!"

As they skirted around the side of Regent's Park, the GPS was telling them to go straight, but a bored policeman was casually waving cars left. Behind him lay a closed-off road—the road through Soho, toward the river and Westminster Abbey.

"We have to go through!" shouted Alfie.

"I KNOW!" screamed Hayley.

She hit the horn, which, being Dean's car, was of course a customized one, and sounded like a bugle playing a cavalry charge. Hayley threw the car onto the sidewalk, around the shocked policeman, and past the barrier.

That was when they heard the first sirens. Blue lights appeared behind them as not one, but three police cars hurtled around the corner. Tourists screamed and dropped their flags as they fled from the path of the wildly swerving car. Hayley leaned hard on the horn, while Alfie waved people out of the way. The heavy *whump-whump* of a police helicopter arrived overhead, and more police cars joined the chase.

As they streaked past roads that led to the parallel Embankment, Alfie caught a glimpse of the Gold State Coach. They were going to make it! Smashing through another set of barriers, they found themselves spinning onto Whitehall, stunned crowds gawking at them from either side. They were ahead of Richard's coach now, with a clear run to the Abbey at Parliament Square.

In theory.

In practice, they now had ten police cars on their tail and two helicopters hovering low, shouting something like "Stop or we open fire!" Oh, and the men with swords on horses. The Blues and Royals were galloping up on either side of the car, swiping at the windows with their ceremonial blades.

SMASH! The back window disappeared in a shower of glass.

"Can't they see who you are?!" yelled Hayley.

"I told them I wasn't coming!" replied Alfie.

Suddenly a police officer in riot gear appeared at the side of the road ahead of them and rolled what looked like a long gray hose across their path. The wheels imploded as they hit the sharp points of the "stinger," and Hayley finally lost control of the car. They spun several times and came to a halt less than two hundred yards from the entrance to the Abbey, where a rather astonished bishop was clutching a hymnbook to his chest like it was body armor.

Alfie and Hayley checked themselves for injuries, but they were both in one piece. For now. Police officers and secret service personnel surrounded the car, pointing their guns and yelling for Alfie and Hayley to show their hands. For a moment Alfie thought they might shoot them before they'd had a chance to surrender. But then Brian came running forward, waving for the security teams to "Stand down!"

The bodyguard leaned into the car and smiled sarcastically. "Alfie! So glad you could make it."

The crumpled spoiler fell off the back of the car and clattered to the ground. Several miles away, watching on TV, Dean Barron let out an anguished cry that led to several neighbors calling the police to report a distressed animal loose on the estate.

• • •

"Impossible! Utterly impossible!"

The Lord Chamberlain was pacing the annex to the Abbey. Alfie had told him everything as fast as he could—what he'd found beneath Professor Lock's study, his suspicion that the final piece of Alfred the Great's crown was here, somewhere in the Abbey, and that the Black Dragon—Lock—planned on finding it. Brian immediately briefed his team with a description of the professor, but so far no one had found him; he was not in his allocated seat. LC insisted that they had already checked the Abbey—it was one of the first places they had looked—the last crown fragment *couldn't* be there.

"You must have missed something," said Alfie.

Outside, Dean's battered car was being loaded onto a recovery vehicle. Soon the road would be cleared and the delayed Gold State Coach would arrive, carrying his brother.

"You have to warn Richard. Is he ready?"

LC and Brian exchanged an awkward glance. Hayley, sitting nearby and nursing a sore ankle, gasped.

"Oh my God. You haven't told him, have you?"

Alfie's blood ran cold. "WHAT?!"

He slumped down on a stone ledge. His poor brother had no idea he was the Defender.

"How could you do that?" Alfie shouted at the Lord Chamberlain.

LC took Alfie by the arm and walked him into a deserted cloister. "I believe there is a reason you were born before your brother."

"It was ten seconds, LC!"

"Ten seconds, ten years, it doesn't matter."

Alfie shook his head. "You've seen how rubbish I am at all this stuff."

Now it was LC's turn to shake his head. "I see a young man who is blind to his true potential, just like Alfred the Great was, a thousand years ago. Alfred was only a young man when he became king. He thought he might rule for a few weeks at most. But he took up that duty and, in the years that followed, he achieved more than he had ever thought possible."

Brian and Hayley appeared at the end of the cloister. LC spoke again, his voice low and urgent.

"The reason I am so hard on you is not because I don't believe in you. It is because I do—very deeply. I want to see you become what you were born to be. It is *your* destiny to rule, not Richard's. Call me old-fashioned—"

"You are. Very," said Alfie.

"*Call me old-fashioned,* but I believe in the line of succession. You were always supposed to rule, whether it's for a few decades or a few hours. You are King Alfred the Second. Who knows? One day, they may even call you *Great.*"

A fanfare sounded from outside the Abbey. The crowds cheered as Richard stepped out of the carriage into the sunshine. It was time to crown a new king.

TWENTY-SEVEN

God Save the King

Princess Eleanor was scared. The coronation had been due to begin half an hour ago, but there were feverish whispers flying through the congregation of a security incident outside, maybe even a terrorist attack. She'd heard the sirens, but now all was quiet again, except for the impatient chattering from the endless ranks of pews behind her. Ellie wasn't the type for praying, but she hoped that Richard was OK. She'd already lost her dad. If anything happened to her brother too . . .

Her mother, Queen Tamara, fidgeted in the seat next to her, pulling her hat low to frustrate the attempts of the TV cameras to see her face. She'd arrived that morning in a cab, straight from the airport, without letting anyone know she was coming. This had resulted in some urgent discussions at the entrance about whether she should be admitted (she wasn't on the guest list, as she hadn't replied to her invitation). But when she gracefully pointed out that refusing entry to the mother of the king might technically qualify as treason, the flustered chief of police had waved her through.

"So Dad's funeral wasn't good enough reason for you to come, but this is?" was how Ellie had greeted her mother when she was shown to the neighboring seat.

"I wanted to be here for Richard," Tamara replied. "And for you."

"Ha!" laughed Ellie sarcastically, turning her back.

The organ boomed out the strident opening notes of the processional march and the air was filled with the soaring voices of the choir. Ellie felt relieved—it was starting; Richard must be fine. But then another wave of murmuring swept through the rows of guests. What had happened? Had some madman sneaked past security? Ellie strained to see. But from her position at the high end of the church, opposite the altar and King Edward's Chair, she still couldn't see Richard. At last, the priests heading the procession appeared through the archway, carrying the shining golden Sword of State and Orb. The excitement among the spectators had reached a peak—*what was going on?* Then Ellie saw the reason for the commotion.

Shuffling up the aisle, dwarfed by the ranks of soldiers on either side, came not Richard, but Alfie! He hitched up his trousers and glanced nervously from side to side, as the coronation guests gawked at him. Ellie stood up in disbelief, catching Alfie's eye. He gave her a small smile and shrug as if to say sorry. Queen Tamara yanked Ellie unceremoniously down into her seat.

"What's he doing? He *abdicated*. He gave it up!" blurted Ellie.

"Looks like he changed his mind," whispered Tamara. "Now smile for the cameras, honey. World's watching, remember?"

Alfie, meanwhile, was trying to stop his trousers from falling down. Minutes earlier he had led a confused Prince Richard into a small side room and explained that he had had a change of heart. He simply couldn't force his brother to take on the heavy duty that by rights was *his* burden. Alfie wanted to be king after all. Richard was speechless with shock at first, then angry. How could Alfie embarrass the family like this? What would people say? Why had he left it so late?

All Alfie could do was keep saying sorry and promise that he would explain everything properly later. But right now, he needed to ask Richard to stand down. Oh, and could he also borrow his clothes? Alfie, in old jeans and scuffed trainers, wasn't exactly dressed for the occasion. And so he had left Richard alone, bewildered, in nothing but his boxer shorts, and made his way into the Abbey wearing a suit that was far too big for him. At the last moment, he had remembered to ask LC about the Crown Jewels—what if they started to glow when he touched them? What would people think?

"Don't worry, Majesty," LC reassured him. "They know where they are. They'll behave themselves."

Now Alfie had to zone it all out. The scandal his return would cause, the difficult questions, the recriminations from friends and family. It would all have to wait. All that mattered now was stopping the Black Dragon. And to do that, Alfie would need his full Defender powers, to have them locked in for good. He needed to be crowned king.

Hayley had never seen the Lord Chamberlain move so fast. The old man was flying along the north side of the Abbey, personally checking every tomb, every memorial, any nook or cranny where the final piece of Alfred's crown could possibly be hidden. But so far he'd found nothing. At the same time, Brian and his team of yeoman warders were discreetly combing the crowds, trying to locate Professor Lock. But with over eight thousand people crammed inside the Abbey, it wasn't going to be easy.

Alfie scanned the sea of faces before him, but he couldn't see his treacherous teacher anywhere. What would he even do if he did spot him? He couldn't exactly interrupt the coronation, stride into the crowd, and arrest him. Then he realized that the Archbishop, who had been standing in front of him droning something in Latin, had stopped talking. The old priest's stern eyes bored into him. Apparently he was waiting for an answer. Alfie could feel his face turning red.

"Sorry," Alfie whispered, "would you mind repeating the question?"

The Archbishop flinched ever so slightly, then calmly spoke. "Will you solemnly promise and swear to govern the people of the United Kingdom of Great Britain and Northern Ireland and her Commonwealth of Nations according to their laws and customs? To punish the wicked and to protect and cherish the just?"

Alfie had heard the oath before, during the rehearsal, but for the first time he felt like perhaps he understood what the words meant. Despite the off-the-charts craziness of the day so far, he found himself really thinking about what he was about to say. The face that flashed into his mind at that moment was not the one he expected—not his brother's, nor his father's, not even LC's. It was the young soldier in Edinburgh, whose name he didn't even know, standing on top of that car, the lava rising toward his feet, his eyes wide with fear and hope as he pleaded with Alfie to save him. And in that split second, Alfie swore to himself that he would never let down someone who needed him ever again. Not that he was suddenly unafraid of getting hurt—he was still terrified—but he had learned over these past few weeks that there were things more important than his own fears. Loyalty. Honor. Friendship. The "duty" that his father had spoken about, which Alfie had always dismissed as just another boring chore, like tidying his room or doing his homework, was in fact something incredibly special. It was a deep, lifelong commitment. It mattered.

Alfie raised his head and spoke with a clear, confident voice: "I solemnly promise so to do."

The rest of the ceremony involved a bewildering array of artifacts, blessings, robes, further oaths, and finally the most sacred part, the Anointing. Four Knights of the Garter brought forward a canopy of golden cloth, which they held over the young king. Underneath, it felt like Alfie's own private little world. The Archbishop took out a golden flask in the shape of an eagle, poured a few drops of strange-smelling oil from it onto the tiny, ancient-looking spoon, and sprinkled it onto Alfie's head. A surge of heat washed over his body like a desert wind. The Abbey seemed to descend into darkness all around him, until he could no longer see anyone or anything except the glowing altar. Then, seemingly from thin air, shimmering apparitions began to float toward him. Visions of kings and queens long past, gray at first, like something from an old movie, then more and more solid, as still further monarchs drifted into vision.

He could hear their voices in his head, though their lips didn't move, a jumble of different languages fading in and out. He saw his grandmother, smiling with kind eyes that he remembered from when he was little. Alfie wasn't scared; it was a warm, pleasant feeling, like he was being filled with light from the feet up, every nerve fizzing, charged up as if by electricity. Finally the voices subsided and his father appeared. His face was free from the furrows of worry and stress that Alfie remembered, his eyes alive with love. He didn't say anything. He didn't need to. He simply kissed Alfie on the forehead and vanished.

Alfie was suddenly back in the Abbey. The canopy had been removed and he was surrounded by curious faces and the low hum of the fidgeting congregation. The Archbishop stood over him holding a crown fringed with dazzling jewels of every color. St. Edward's Crown had been worn by generations of his family at their coronations, and now it was his turn. The Archbishop lowered the crown onto Alfie's head. It was heavy, but Alfie remained upright, still as a statue. He was more than a boy now. He was a part of history: a king.

Maybe the Lord Chamberlain was right. Maybe this was meant to be.

A guttural laugh echoed around the Abbey. It seemed to be coming from above, somewhere high up in the vaulted ceiling. A jolt of alarm swept through the people on the church floor as they gazed up into the dark recesses of the roof. A scream rang out, and the large lady in the peach hat pointed up at a grand stained-glass window depicting St. George's mythical slaying of the dragon. Suddenly the shape of the dragon unfurled and crawled across the window and onto the wall. Alfie could see it clearly now, the Black Dragon, its scaly tail flicking across the stonework.

"Do you think just because you wear a crown, that makes you a king?"

The Black Dragon's mocking tone rang out across the Abbey. The creature launched itself off the wall and landed with a crack of marble in the central aisle. Hysterical screams rang out as the guests descended into panic, streaming out of the pews and running for the doors like water draining from a bath. Bravely, the soldiers lining the aisle drew their swords and closed ranks between the fearsome beast and the royal party. But the

Black Dragon merely stooped and swung its tail in a broad arc, knocking them off their feet and carving a way through.

Alfie yelled to his mother to get Ellie out, tossed the crown he was wearing onto the chair, and ran to the altar, risking a look behind him.

The Black Dragon beat back another group of soldiers with a torrent of fiery breath. It stepped up to King Edward's Chair and kicked it over, like it was flipping a deckchair. The Archbishop cowered as the Black Dragon spun its tail high and brought it crunching down. But instead of hitting the priest, it struck the Stone of Destiny—the ancient rock that had arrived from Scotland the day before, to take its traditional place beneath the Coronation Chair. It crumbled under the impact, and as he peered at it, Alfie thought he could make out something glistening amid the rubble.

The Black Dragon reached down and lifted out a dusty piece of curved gold, embossed with jewels. The last fragment of Alfred the Great's lost crown! The dragon pulled the rest of the reassembled crown from beneath its scales and discarded the bones that bridged the final gap. Alfie watched, horrified, as the Black Dragon brought the fragment from the stone and the rest of the crown together. The gold edges seemed to melt into each other and re-form before his eyes.

The beast laughed once more. "Now let me show you what *real* power looks like . . ."

The Black Dragon raised the crown and placed it on its head. Alfie shielded his eyes as a searing white light burst out. The dragon roared so loudly that masonry cracked and fell from the ceiling, pews toppled like dominoes, and the banners draped all around the Abbey fluttered to the floor like dead leaves. When Alfie looked again, the Black Dragon seemed to have grown even larger. Fire burned in its eyes, smoke billowed from its horned nostrils, and flames licked across its scales as if it were made of fire. It leaned forward, shaking and convulsing, until, with a hideous snap, *wings* exploded from its back. The Black Dragon screeched and flapped its black, leathery wings for the first time, rising into the air like some newborn creature of hell.

Terrified guests were still trying to flee the Abbey through the mass of people at the main doors. Some lay injured in the melee. Courageous soldiers pulled each other up and prepared for another assault on the intruder. Alfie knew they would die if he didn't do something. He gripped the sword and readied himself to charge. The Black Dragon tilted its wings, spun to face him, and opened its jaws.

Brian collided with Alfie, pushing him clear as the jet of flames ignited the altar behind them. Alfie felt other hands tugging him—Hayley and LC, bundling him away. He didn't want to go, but they pulled him through a door and into an empty side chapel, just as another fireball erupted at his back. Brian slammed the door behind them and leaned against it, sucking in air.

"What are you doing?" yelled Alfie. "There are people still in there!"

LC, breathless and pale, laid his hand on Alfie's shoulder. "Yes, and you will help them . . . Hayley!"

Hayley held out the Shroud Tunic. "What do you say we even the odds a bit?"

She helped Alfie slip the tunic over his head, and his Defender armor unfurled. Swiftly, Brian helped him fix his spurs and load his Sword of State and other weapons onto his belt. Now LC was holding out something else for Alfie. The Ring of Command. Its ruby seemed to pulse with energy as the old man slid it onto Alfie's finger. It felt tight and reassuringly heavy. It glowed with a deep red light.

"What do I do? How do I use it?" asked Alfie.

"Sorry, matey, there's no training for this one," said Brian. "Hold up your hand and think like a king."

From the other side of the door they could hear the roaring of the Black Dragon and the rush of fire taking hold.

LC gripped Alfie by the shoulders and looked into his eyes. "You must remove Alfred's crown from the dragon's head before it fuses with it forever. Do you understand?"

The Lord Chamberlain knelt. Brian followed suit.

"No, you don't need to," stuttered Alfie.

LC and Brian looked to Hayley, waiting for her to join them. But she just shot them a withering look and held out her fist to Alfie. He smiled as he bumped it back.

The Lord Chamberlain sighed, then cried out, "God save the king!"

"GOD SAVE THE KING!" shouted Brian and Hayley.

"Now go kick that dragon's butt, Alfie!" Hayley added.

- TWENTY-EIGHT -

Battle Royal

Princess Eleanor and Queen Tamara never made it to the exit. In the chaos, Tamara had twisted her ankle. Although she told Ellie to go on alone, her daughter had insisted on helping, pulling her down into the choir stalls just before the Black Dragon started spraying fire in all directions. They were still lying there now, trying not to make a sound, in case the beast heard them. Slowly, Ellie craned her neck to peek underneath the stalls. They would have to make a run for it soon—the fire was spreading fast—but Ellie didn't fancy bumping into that creature along the way.

CRRRRRACK!

The stalls they were hiding behind were wrenched from their moorings and cast aside with a smash of splintering wood. The Black Dragon hovered right above, its beating wings fanning the flames that surrounded them. Tamara threw herself in front of her daughter, shielding her as best she could. The dragon opened its jaws, the glow of flames growing in its throat.

A blinding white light filled the Abbey, and Ellie and Tamara looked up, astonished to see the Defender deflecting the Black Dragon's fire with his glowing sword. Mother and daughter clung to each other as they dashed for safety, keeping low and running for the south door. But Ellie couldn't help pausing for a moment and looking back at the incredible sight—the Defender versus the Black Dragon, locked in a fight to the death.

Alfie knew he had to keep moving if he was to have any chance. He could already feel how much greater the Black Dragon's power had become since it had put on King Alfred's crown.

"Spurs!" he yelled, and Wyvern rolled out beneath him, braying fiercely as she carried him high into the air. They weaved from side to side as the pursuing dragon's fireballs crackled against the ornate ceiling, bringing down yet more huge chunks of stone. If he could separate the crown from the dragon, it might weaken it.

Yeah, but to do that I have to get close enough to him without being flame-grilled first, he thought. It wasn't much of a plan, but at least the Defender's appearance had given the soldiers time to evacuate the last of the guests.

Something smacked into the back of the Defender's head with the force of a train. The Black Dragon, tired of spitting fire at him, had resorted to a good old-fashioned flying kick. Alfie tumbled head over heels as Wyvern shrank back into his spurs. He crash-landed into a large brass lectern, bending it beyond repair. The Black Dragon thumped to the floor, its claws shattering the marble, and pressed home its attack, smacking the Defender from one side of the aisle to the other with vicious swipes of its barbed tail.

"Do you really think you can save them? The people. You've saved no one," hissed the creature.

Alfie struck back with his sword, but each blow seemed to glance off his opponent without even slowing it down. The dragon was too strong now. Maybe reasoning with it would help.

"I know it's you, Professor. It's not too late to stop this. No one needs to get hurt."

Alfie summoned his shield just in time as the Black Dragon belched another jet of flames over him. *Then again, maybe not . . .*

"You know nothing," bellowed the Black Dragon. "All you need to call me now is your KING!"

Alfie pinned his back to a column as more flames crackled all around him. On his finger the Ring of Command was glowing gently. *Oh well,* thought Alfie, *nothing quite like learning on the job.* He peered around the column and pointed his clenched fist at the heavy pews that lay in a heap to one side of the aisle. Nothing happened. Nothing, that is, apart from the column at his back exploding into rubble as the dragon's wing scythed through it inches above his head.

Alfie rolled clear, diving behind the next column. *One more try.* He reached out again with his fist, focusing on the pile of benches. He did his best to shut out the dark shape of the Black Dragon stalking toward him. This time, to his surprise, Alfie could feel the benches react to his thoughts. It was as if the centuries-old oak itself was talking back to him, answering his command. A thick pew leapt from the floor and spun toward the Black Dragon. It shattered against its scales and it bellowed in pain. *Yes!*

Alfie sent another pew spearing through the air, but this time the Black Dragon was ready and caught it. It considered the Defender for a moment, as if impressed. But the underhand strike had only angered it more. Using the pew like a battering ram, it hurled it into the Defender's chest.

CRUNCH. Alfie's armor saved his ribs from being shattered, but now he was trapped beneath the bench. Alfie tried to command the pew to move again, but the dragon's foot was on it, grinding it against him. Alfie felt panic taking hold. If he couldn't calm himself, then he couldn't use his powers, and if he couldn't do that . . .

A whistle rang out, and the Black Dragon turned

to see Hayley at the other end of the aisle. She ran in a wide arc, as fast as she could, from column to column, as the dragon sprayed a jet of fire, just missing her.

Brian popped out from behind a stone pillar and unloaded a full clip of bullets into the Black Dragon's back. Sparks flew off its scales as the creature's head snapped around. The distraction worked. Now free of the pew, Alfie could see the Black Dragon's back was turned, but it had Brian cornered—in a few seconds it would be on him. Looking at the weapons on his belt, Alfie had an idea. He hadn't trained much with the Scepters, but he'd seen what they could do.

He whipped out the pair of long gold sticks, joined by a shimmering thread so thin it was hardly visible. Alfie spun them around his head like a ninja wielding nunchakus. He took aim and tossed them straight at the back of the Black Dragon's head. The Scepters found their target, the silver thread slicing between the beast's head and Alfred's crown, separating them and sending the crown rolling away across the floor. The Black Dragon bellowed with rage and stumbled, giving Brian enough time to back off.

The Black Dragon dived for the crown, reaching out a clawed hand, but Hayley streaked past it and swept the crown off the floor. She sprinted to the exit and handed it to the Lord Chamberlain, who rushed it away, protected by a phalanx of yeoman warders. The dragon roared and flapped its wings, starting to take off again, spewing fire in all directions.

Now or never, thought Alfie. He raced down the aisle, leapt, and swung his sword down with all his strength, severing one of the Black Dragon's wings. The monster shrieked in pain, crashing down into the altar and lashing out with its claws. Alfie circled around, careful to keep his distance from the whipping tail. But he could see that the dragon was hurt. This was the only chance he would get. He gripped the sword with both hands, raised his arms, and dived toward the prone figure of his enemy.

Pain exploded through Alfie's body. He lost his grip on the sword and it clattered to the floor. The Black Dragon had unfurled its remaining wing and impaled Alfie's hand with the spike at its end. Alfie screamed out, every nerve ending on fire, as he grabbed at his hand in vain. The Black Dragon rose, lifting Alfie off his feet. With a roar, the creature threw him down. Alfie looked at his injured hand in horror—black lines were spreading out from the raw wound, filling his veins. *Poison,* thought Alfie, struggling to focus. The agony coursing through his limbs was almost too much to bear.

Flames licked high up the stone walls on either side. Gold from the tombs was melting in the intense heat and pouring out into the nave. The sound of buckling metal and cracking wood was deafening. Soon the inferno would take hold so strongly that it could never be brought under control. The Defender knelt in the shadow of the Black Dragon, his head bowed, arms behind his back, his breathing shallow.

"Yes, kneel before your new king. Kneel, as all those outside these walls will soon kneel to me."

Slowly Alfie brought his right hand forward. The Ring of Command glowed searchlight-bright through the swirling, choking smoke. Alfie's voice was quiet but firm. "*Non ducor, duco.* I am not led, I lead."

The Black Dragon turned to see a huge shape hovering above it—a massive block of stone, marble, and gold—St. Edward the Confessor's entire tomb had left the ground and was floating over its head. Straining to keep it under his command, Alfie opened his fist and rolled to the side. The Black Dragon made a grab for him, but missed, its scaly arm outstretched. A fiery shriek broke from its lips as tons of ancient rock plummeted down like an avalanche, burying it.

The doors to the Abbey flew open and firemen in breathing apparatuses burst in, hosing down the flames. In the shadows, Alfie lay motionless against a blackened pillar. His spurs glowed and Wyvern emerged, lifting him up onto her back. She turned her neck, nuzzling her master's face and whinnying softly. Taking off, she flew to the back of the Abbey and landed next to LC. The old man lifted Alfie's hand—the poison where he had been impaled was eating away at the flesh, black lines spreading beneath the skin.

"Brian!" he called.

The armorer came running, with Hayley by his side. He was carrying another sword—the one with the blunted, square tip. They placed it in Alfie's limp hand. "Majesty, you must hold the Sword of Mercy. Only you can make it work."

But there was no response from beneath the Defender's armor. Hayley stepped forward, close to tears . . . and whacked the side of the Defender's helmet hard with her hand. "WAKE UP, ALFIE!"

Alfie's grip tightened. Suddenly the Sword of Mercy began to glow. He groaned and sat up as the wound in his palm closed over. He was healed. With a relieved snort, Wyvern disappeared into the spurs and the others caught Alfie as he fell. The young king reached up and removed his armor. His dazed face was red with sweat. "I dreamed someone hit me," he murmured.

Hayley laughed. "Yeah, sorry about that."

Alfie turned to LC. "Can kings ever name themselves?" he asked.

"I don't see why not, sir. What did you have in mind?"

"Alfie the Not So Bad. What do you think?" the new king croaked. And then he passed out.

• • •

Hours later, long after Brian had carried Alfie to the waiting car and rushed him back to the palace, a recovery team of yeoman warders pulled away the cracked rubble of St. Edward the Confessor's tomb to reveal the figure lying underneath. The Black Dragon was gone. In its place lay Professor Lock—small, naked, and black with dust and soot. The chief yeoman warder checked his pulse.

"My God . . . he's alive."

- TWENTY-NINE -

Uneasy Lies the Head
That Wears a Crown

Superheroes were real.

It was all anyone at the coronation banquet could talk about. Four hundred places were laid for the most important guests—foreign kings and queens, prime ministers and presidents, famous business leaders and celebrities. The gate-crashing of the coronation by the Black Dragon was the sole topic of conversation. *What was it? Was it gone now? Was it true that the Defender had turned up, saved the king, and killed the creature?* Footage of the battle filmed by one of the TV cameras that hadn't been destroyed was watched and rewatched. The prime minister had already made an emergency statement—she was "determined to get to the bottom of it" and promised to "find out what threat these mysterious figures pose to the nation."

Alfie had lost his appetite. He didn't think that going ahead with the banquet was really appropriate after what had happened, but LC had insisted.

No one was badly hurt, most of the Abbey had been saved, and the rest would be rebuilt. Besides, the country needed to see their new king going about business as usual in these "unusual times."

At least in all the fuss, Alfie's change of heart was already old news. Even his sister seemed to have forgiven him, though Ellie said she still thought he was a total dingbat for rocking up at the last minute like that. She was just glad they'd all gotten out alive. Ellie had even insisted on sitting next to her mother. The Lord Chamberlain did not look happy when he spotted Queen Tamara sitting at the top table—Alfie got the feeling there was no love lost between them.

His mother hadn't stayed long. However, before she left, she took Alfie aside for a moment.

"Alfie, what you asked me on the phone," she said. "I do know what you were talking about, but I couldn't say—you never know who is listening. I have so much to tell you. Come and see me soon, OK, sweetie?"

She kissed Alfie and left before he could ask her what she meant. But he promised himself he would make the trip to her ranch soon and find out.

Alfie had insisted that Hayley be admitted to the banquet, even though she wasn't on the guest list. He'd found her a seat next to the king of Sweden and another surprise guest . . . Hayley's gran. The old woman was in royal heaven. She insisted Hayley take a photograph of every inch of the lavish table, as well as selfies with most of the guests. Herne trotted over and rested his head on the old lady's lap, receiving a slice of venison for his trouble.

As Alfie passed by, greeting his guests, Hayley jumped up from the table and gave him a kiss on the cheek. "Nice work today, Your Maj," she said.

Brian coughed as he strolled past. "Hands off the king, please, miss, or I might have to lock you up in the Tower."

Alfie and Hayley giggled and went back to their seats.

The only person still missing was Richard. Alfie wasn't surprised—his brother could handle almost anything, but the humiliation of being replaced at the last minute must have stung. *What if he never forgives me?* Alfie was already terrified by what he'd just taken on—the double life, king *and* Defender. But doing that without his brother to lean on when he needed him? Alfie hated the idea.

The Lord Chamberlain clinked a fork against his glass and brought the room to attention. "Your Majesties and Highnesses, my lords, ladies, and esteemed guests. I am delighted to announce the revival of a custom long forgotten, but one that I believe is rather apt for the occasion. Please be upstanding for . . . the king's champion!"

The doors were flung open, and a majestic black stallion cantered in with a clatter of hooves, ridden by a knight in armor. Squeals of surprise and alarm filled the ballroom, but were quickly replaced with laughter and cheers as the knight lifted his visor. It was Prince Richard. Smiling, he unfurled a scroll and declared:

"If any person shall deny our Sovereign Lord Alfred, King of the United Kingdom of Great Britain and Northern Ireland, to be the right heir to the Imperial Crown of this Realm, here is his champion, who saith that he lieth, and is a false traitor, being ready in person to combat with him, on what day soever he shall be appointed. God save the king!"

The guests roared their approval and took up the chant. Richard dismounted, approached the top table, and knelt in front of his brother. Alfie felt like crying with relief and happiness. But he thought blubbering like a baby probably wasn't the sort of thing a new king should do, so instead he stepped forward, pulled Richard to his feet, and gave him a hug. "No hard feelings, Richie?"

"Are you kidding? I reckon you saved my life back there. Just try not to leave it so late next time.

And I wouldn't mind my trousers back . . . Dad would be proud of you today, Alfie."

The doors to the balcony had been opened, and Alfie could hear more chanting from the thousands gathered outside the palace gates on the Mall.

"We want the king! We want the king!"

He couldn't believe it. Were they really saying that for *him*? Richard gave him a friendly nudge and told him he'd better go outside quickly, before they changed their minds. But first, Alfie needed to speak to the Lord Chamberlain. He took the old man aside and whispered to him. "What about Alfred's crown? Where is it?"

"In a safe place."

"And the Black Dragon? Professor Lock?"

"He is being taken somewhere he can't do any harm."

Satisfied, Alfie turned back to the balcony. But then he stopped, suddenly panicked. "What do I say to them?"

The old man thought for a moment and smiled. "Something from the heart, Majesty."

Alfie nodded, took a deep breath, and went outside to greet his people.

- THIRTY -

Traitors' Gate

The small rowing boat passed unnoticed beneath London Bridge. The prisoner sat, head bowed in silence, just as he had ever since he'd regained consciousness seven days after the battle in the Abbey. After the yeoman warders had spirited Professor Lock away to a secret military hospital, their doctors had run an exhaustive series of tests on his body. They had all come back normal.

The beast that resided inside him was gone, cast out, they said, by the trauma of his defeat at the hands of the Defender and his separation from Alfred the Great's stolen crown, the source of his power.

The shackles hanging heavy around his wrists and ankles made any thoughts of swimming for shore impossible. Even if he did try to escape, the escort of four yeoman warders would soon stop him.

"Count yourself lucky, mate," said the beefeater at the prow, nodding back at the bridge. "Few hundred years ago your head would've been up there on a spike."

"Best place for it, if you ask me," chuckled one of the beefeaters, pulling the oars.

The boat glided toward the north bank and under the low arch of Traitors' Gate. Lock knew the names of every rogue and backstabber that had been brought to the Tower of London by this very same route over the centuries. Part of him was proud to be counted among them. But he knew all he had to look forward to now was a life sentence in the deepest of the fortress's dungeons. No one would ever find out where he had gone or why. The name of Professor Cameron Lock would not even be a footnote in the history books.

As the boat docked inside the walls of the Tower grounds, a ripple moved across the river's surface, disturbing the moon's reflection. The beefeater at the stern leaned over the side and peered into the water. He knew there were some fair-sized fish to be found in the moat. Perhaps it was—

SPLASH!

A hulking black shape burst from the water, hurling the beefeater overboard. The Black Dragon heaved itself onto the boat. For a moment, the remaining guards were frozen in shock. How could the monster be here? Lock was supposed to be the Black Dragon. It was impossible. They scrambled for their weapons, but too slow—a gale of fire erupted from the dragon's jaws and swept over them. Two fell screaming into the river. The last, the captain, though also in flames, attacked anyway, thrusting his pike at the giant beast. The razor-sharp tip of a scaly tail impaled him with a sickening squelch, and as it withdrew, he crumpled to the deck, dead.

The Black Dragon stood over Professor Lock, its mutated reptilian body glistening wet. The stump where the Defender had severed its right wing was still raw on its back. It extended a long claw and sliced through Lock's shackles as if they were tissue paper. Lock spoke even and clear, as a parent would to a child. "I was beginning to think you weren't coming."

"You took my place at the Abbey. I repay my debts," growled the beast.

At least that part of the plan worked, thought Lock. Everyone believed he was the Black Dragon. Part of him couldn't wait for them to find out who it really was beneath the monster's scales. That would wipe the smile off the young king's face.

The creature snarled and lifted Lock off his feet by the scruff of his neck. "Why am I still like this? You said it was only temporary."

"The crown's power sealed the dragon's blood inside you. I can reverse it, but first we have a war to win. You still want the throne, don't you?"

Suddenly the Black Dragon coughed and released its grip on Lock. It fell to its knees, convulsing and groaning as it transformed. Bones cracked as they shrank and claws disappeared back into its hands. Scales withdrew, replaced by pink skin. In a matter of seconds, it was human once again, crouched naked and shaking on the deck of the boat. His voice was hoarse but firm.

"Yes, Professor. I still want what you promised me. What should be mine."

The young man raised his face into the moonlight, hair slick with sweat, eyes burning red with anger.

"I want the throne," said Prince Richard.

- ACKNOWLEDGMENTS -

We would like to thank our parents, for reading to us, for filling our homes with books, and for not laughing (too much) when we said this was what we wanted to do for a living. Special thanks to Linda Huckerby for teaching her nephew to read (Tim and Tobias have a lot to answer for!).

We would like to thank the English and history teachers who encouraged us to be creative and curious about the past, especially Jim McNicholas, Allen Ramsden, Hugh Clifton, Peter Knox, Richard Aldrich, and Mr. Prentice. Thanks also go to all the family, friends, and professionals who listened to us pitch an outlandish story about superheroes and kings and monsters and who gave feedback on our first attempt at writing something that wasn't a script, especially Paula Rosenthal for her early encouragement.

We owe a huge debt to our ever-supportive and indomitable agent Cathy King and her fantastic team at Independent Talent Group—Ikenna Obiekwe, Alex Rusher, and Sam Kingston-Jones—for their tireless work on our behalf. Extra thanks to Anna Huckerby for her exceptional and speedy initial proofreading and for testing bits out on her class, and to the amazing Peter Matthews, Emily Lamm, and Jamie Gregory, Zack Clark, and the whole team at Scholastic for throwing themselves into our world with such enthusiasm and expertise. We are eternally grateful for the stellar work of Tom Percival on the UK book cover, and Carol Ly and Matt Rockefeller for the US cover.

Above all, our heartfelt thanks are due to that true king and Defender, our editor David Maybury, without whose total belief, good humor, and pretty much constant Skype messages, you would not be reading this and we would not be having half as much fun writing it.

NICK OSTLER AND **MARK HUCKERBY** are Emmy Award–winning and BAFTA-nominated screen-writers best known for writing popular TV shows such as *Danger Mouse, Thunderbirds Are Go!* and *Peter Rabbit. Defender of the Realm* is their first novel.

www.defenderoftherealm.co.uk

Visit their website
www.ostlerandhuckerby.com